A MESSAGE FROM CHICKEN HOUSE

I've really enjoyed Christopher Edge's other brilliant books – in fact, I've often thought his jokes were *out of this world*. So when Dr Sarah Ryan won our Big Idea competition with an idea about an alien parent (aren't all parents aliens?), Christopher seemed a natural fit. And if you ask me, he knows an awful lot about outer space . . . I wonder if he's ever visited? Anyway, this story is closer to home than all that. At heart it's about how, wherever we come from, family is oddly and tremendously important.

BARRY CUNNINGHAM
Publisher
Chicken House

SPACE ODDITY

CHRISTOPHER EDGE

2 PALMER STREET,
FROME, SOMERSET
BA11 1DS

Text © Christopher Edge 2021
From an original idea by Sarah Ryan © The Big Idea Competition Limited
Illustrations © Ben Mantle 2021

First published in Great Britain in 2021
Chicken House
2 Palmer Street
Frome, Somerset BA11 1DS
United Kingdom
www.chickenhousebooks.com

Designed and typeset by Steve Wells
Printed and bound in Great Britain by CPI Group (UK) Ltd, Croydon CR0 4YY

The paper used in this Chicken House book is made from wood grown
in sustainable forests.

1 3 5 7 9 10 8 6 4 2

British Library Cataloguing in Publication data available.

ISBN 978-1-912626-86-1
eISBN 978-1-913322-50-2

For Josie, who's always
the first to spot the stars.

And in memory of
David Bowie,
whose songs told us that
we're not alone.

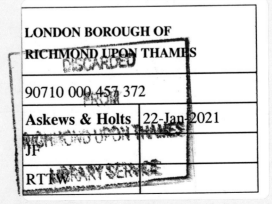

'I'm sure the universe is full of intelligent life. It's just been too intelligent to come here.'

ARTHUR C. CLARKE

TWELVE YEARS AGO ...

A SHOOTING STAR

It looked like a shooting star at first – a silver streak of light, glowing bright against the darkness of the night. And trailing in its wake soared three more glowing spheres, their lights flashing blue and white as they fell towards Middlewich Forest.

But if anyone could have heard the noise coming from inside the silver streak of light they would have realized that this wasn't a shooting star – it was a *screaming* star.

'*AAAAAAAARRRRGGGHHHHHH!!!*'

The alien's scream faded into a gibber of fear as he spun around the observation dome. Branches and leaves bounced off the flying saucer's failing force field as the spacecraft crashed through the trees. On the rear-view screen he could see the glowing spheres growing even brighter, their blue-white beams of light almost blinding him as they closed in for the kill.

'WARNING! YOU ARE TRESPASSING IN A COSMIC ZONE OF EXCLUSION. ALL TRAVEL IS STRICTLY RESTRICTED. WARNING! YOU HAVE ENTERED THE ATMOSPHERE OF A P-CLASS PLANET. ALL CONTACT IS STRICTLY FORBIDDEN. WARNING! YOUR VESSEL WILL BE VAPORIZED IN THREE ZEPTONS. PREPARE FOR DISINTEGRATION, ION OF MMBOG—'

With a despairing flick of his wrist, Ion tried to cut the communication channel into silence. For an alien, Ion looked remarkably human. One head, two arms, two legs. No tentacles. The only thing that would make him stand out from the crowd, apart from his shiny silver jumpsuit, was the colour of his skin – which was a bright shade of green.

Ion grabbed hold of the starry egg that hung suspended in the air in front of him. This was the Quintessence – the beating heart of his spaceship. With this he could control everything: the interstellar drive, the quantum gravity boosters and the Zeno cloaking shield. But all of these were useless now . . .

Wrenching the egg-shaped device free from the energy matrix, Ion's emerald fingers scrabbled to activate the emergency settings. If he couldn't save his spaceship, he could still save himself. Through the observation dome, Ion could see the ground of this strange planet racing up to meet him. The only chance he had left was an emergency teleport to the surface of this world. And there wasn't far to go.

Twisting the device, Ion heard the lifeboat mode load with a click. The stars that shimmered across the Quintessence's surface now shone with a pale green glow. As this eerie light surrounded him, Ion felt the atoms in his body start to unravel.

The last thing he heard was the sound of the robotic voice ringing in his ear: **'YOUR VESSEL WILL BE VAPORIZED IN ONE ZEPTON–'**

And then he was gone.

JAKE, I AM YOUR FATHER

'**E**XTERMINATE! EXTERMINATE!'
I flatten myself against the intergalactic scenery as the Year Five Daleks sweep past me in the wings. The cheers and applause that greeted their synchronized dance routine to the *Doctor Who* theme tune is still ringing across the school hall.

The last of the Daleks pokes his sink plunger into my chest as he passes me by. 'Primitive life form detected! Exterminate!'

'Get lost, tinhead.' The Wookie standing

next to me swats the Dalek away with a swipe of her paw.

'Ow, Amba,' the Dalek protests, tinfoil and egg boxes flapping as he beats a hasty retreat. 'That really hurt!'

'Put a sock in it, Lucas,' Amba says, flicking the woolly fringe of her Chewbacca costume out of her eyes. 'Are you OK, Jake?'

'I'm fine,' I reply, wishing that I'd been the one to tell Lucas to get lost.

'You should've told him to put a sock on it,' Damon chips in, his voice muffled behind his Darth Vader helmet. 'That's the best way to defeat a Dalek. Stick a sock on their eyestalk and they can't see a thing. For a master race of alien monsters, they're pretty rubbish really.'

Amba laughs and even I can't stop myself from smiling at the thought of Darth Vader using his smelly socks to beat the Daleks.

Everyone in school is dressed up like this because of the theme of this year's concert.

OAKWOOD PRIMARY SCHOOL PRESENTS

A GLITTERING CELEBRATION OF

SPACE

AND THE

STARS

So far this evening we've had the Wind Band's medley of songs about the Moon, a Search for a Star talent show, the Guitar Orchestra performing 'Across the Universe' and the Year Five Dance Group's celebration of all things *Doctor Who*. Now the school choir are back on the stage singing 'Space Oddity'.

This is my dad's favourite song. It's by this singer called David Bowie who used to pretend to be an alien. Dad's always playing me his old videos on YouTube as he tries to get me to sing along. David Bowie did look kind of strange sometimes, but he wasn't really an alien. Dad says he was a star.

That's what Dad wants to be – a rock star. He spends most of his time at home playing air guitar and pulling rock star shapes as he blasts his music loud. Dad's real name is Ion Jones, but he says his stage name is going to be Ion Cosmos. He's got this crazy idea that he's going to be the biggest star in the universe.

There's only one problem.

He can't sing.

Mum doesn't seem to mind that Dad's singing voice sounds like a cat being strangled to death. She just makes gooey eyes at him when he serenades her with 'Space Oddity' for the zillionth time. Dad says it's their song as it reminds him of the time when he first met my mum, staring up at the stars while she stole his heart. That's when I tell them to pass me the sick bag.

Standing at the side of the stage, I peer through a gap in the scenery to see if I can spot Mum and Dad in the audience. The school hall is packed, but I spot Mum straightaway. She's sitting in the very front row, dressed in her paramedic's uniform. She must have come to the concert as soon as her shift on the ambulance finished.

Mum has a proper job helping people – unlike Dad. Whatever job he tries, he never gets it right. Like that time he worked at the supermarket and got into a fight with one of the self-service checkouts. Dad said it was trying to vaporize him and zapped it with his pricing gun, but it was only telling him that there was an unauthorized item in its bagging area. This got Dad his final warning, so when he accidentally crashed the line of shopping trolleys he was collecting into a special offer display of baked beans and pasta shapes, the manager sacked him on the spot. Most people would be sad about losing their job, but not my dad. He just came home with a big smile on his face and seventy-six badly dented tins of Alphabetti spaghetti.

Giving Mum a wave, I spot that the seat next to her is empty. I look around, but there's no sign of Dad. He must've popped to the toilet or something.

As the choir sings out the final word of the song, the audience breaks into applause.

'Get ready, Gym Stars,' Mrs Mays says as she appears at the side of the stage. 'You're on next.'

Mrs Mays takes us for gym club after school. That's where Amba, Damon and me became friends – at Gym Stars. At first, I wasn't even thinking of doing gymnastics, but when it came to picking an after-school club, there wasn't really much choice. Chess Club, Drama

Club and Forest Skills were all full, Cooking Club was cancelled because Mrs Fitz had food poisoning, and Times Tables Fun Club was just Extra Maths in disguise. So when Damon and Amba asked, 'Are you coming to Gym Stars?' I just said 'yes' straightaway.

I didn't even know I could do gymnastics. I've always had a bit of a spring in my step and sometimes other kids make fun of my bouncy walk, but it turns out that when it comes to gymnastics a spring in your step is just what you need. From that very first practice, I found I could jump higher, flip further and tumble faster than anyone else in the club – even Amba, and she's been doing gymnastics since she was six. Mrs Mays says it's like I forget that gravity exists when I get on the gymnastics mat.

That's why I'm dressed as Luke Skywalker now, ready to take the starring role in this *Star Wars* gymnastics routine that Mrs Mays has worked out for us. We've been practising for weeks, but I still feel a nervous fizz in the pit of my stomach as the lights go down and the choir shuffle their way off the stage.

'Good luck,' Amba whispers as Mrs Mays shepherds us into our positions.

Then the stage lights go up and the *Star Wars* music starts and I've not got time to be worried any more.

BAAAAH–BAHHH! BA–BA–BA–BAAAA-AAH–BAH! BA–BA–BA–BAAAAAAH–BAH! BA–BA–BA–BAAAAAAAHHHHH!

Ewoks start their tumbling passes from opposite sides of the stage, their furry flips and twists followed by forward rolls. Amba was meant to dress up as an Ewok too but, seeing as she's so much taller than everyone else in the class, Mrs Mays decided to turn her woolly costume into Chewbacca instead.

Now it's her turn to strike a pose in the centre of the stage. Leaning forward on her paws, Amba swings her long legs round in a circle, the toes of her furry boots pointing upwards as she ends the flair with a flourish. Pushing herself up on to her feet, Amba stretches her arms out and then kicks into a run, letting out a Wookie roar as she cartwheels off the other side of the stage.

As the audience applaud and the music swirls, I take a deep breath.

It's time for me to make my grand entrance.

Taking a few quick steps, I bound forward on to the stage as I launch myself into my first tumbling run. As I push myself off the ground, it almost feels like the Force is pulsing through me, my body twisting acrobatically as I soar through the air.

OOOOHHHHH!

As I land, I leap forward again, somersaulting head over heels. I flip back and bounce in an aerial twist, then land with an acrobatic roll.

AAAAHHHHH!

Bounding to my feet, I start my last tumbling run with a backward take-off. I flip, twist and roll, every backwards bounce sending me higher still, arms and legs stretching out as I hang in the air for a second or two. It almost feels like I'm flying.

Then I pull off the perfect landing, a beam on my face as I peer out into the audience.

Through the bright lights shining down from the rafters, I see my mum clapping wildly, the smile on her face as big as my own. But the seat next to her is still empty, with no sign of Dad.

I feel my smile fade a little.

Typical. He's missed my big moment again.

Then, with a trumpet blare, the music suddenly changes into something more sinister.

DAH–DAH–DAH DUM–DA DAH–DUM–DAH–DA – DAAAAAHHHH!

Glancing to the wings, I hold out my hand as Mrs Mays tosses me my lightsaber.

It's time for the grand finale.

Pressing the button on its side, I flick my wrist to extend the lightsaber and watch it light up with a metallic swoosh. As the blue blade glows, I turn to face the spot where Damon should be standing, dressed as Darth Vader.

*DAH–DAH–DAH DUM–DA DAH–DUM–
DAH–DA – DAAAAAHHHH!*

There's no sign of him there.

Puzzled, I glance around to where my teacher is still standing in the wings. Mrs Mays looks just as confused as me. Then her eyes open wide in surprise as the music suddenly stops to be replaced by the mechanical rasp of Darth Vader's breath.

KKKKHHHHH! HHHHSSSSS!

Feeling relieved, I spin round with a grin, ready to face Damon at last. We've spent ages choreographing this fight scene, but I almost drop my lightsaber in shock as Darth Vader somersaults on to the stage.

I say Darth Vader, but it actually looks more like Darth *Lamer*.

He's wearing a black plastic bin on his head; a badly drawn Darth Vader mask scrawled on the front of this in silver pen. And as his black cape billows, the strange figure swings his red lightsaber in a swooping arc.

SCHURMMMMMM!

I scramble backwards, unable to believe what I'm seeing, as Darth Lamer's lightsaber swings towards me again. Throwing my arm up, my own lightsaber just blocks the blow, the blue and red blades clashing with a fizzing hiss.

VRRUMMMUMMM! FVISH!

This isn't part of the routine we practised, but then this can't be Damon beneath the bin helmet. He's only in Year Six like me and this idiot's as tall as a grown-up.

KKKKHHHHHH! HHHHSSSSS!

'Jake,' the voice rasps with a metallic hiss. 'I am your father.'

Oh no. This can't be happening.

Still backing away, I catch my foot on the edge of the mat. My arms windmill wildly as I feel myself falling backwards, but it's too late to save myself as I land on my bottom.

Everyone laughs and my face flushes red.

It's all gone wrong and I know the reason why.

Standing over me, the dark figure reaches up to lift the bin off his head and I see the face behind the mask.

It's not Darth Vader – it's my dad!

The dyed-green tuft in his blond spiky hair that he reckons makes him look cool is now flattened to his forehead with sweat, but Dad's blue-green eyes shine bright with excitement as a girl's voice calls out from the choir, 'It's Jake's dad!'

There's a cheer from the audience and then every kid in the hall joins in the chant.

'Jake's dad! Jake's dad! Jake's dad!'

With a windmilling wave of his lightsaber, Dad reaches out a hand to help me up, but I roughly push this away.

'Jake?' he asks with a puzzled look on his face. 'Are you OK?'

I shake my head as I climb to my feet.

'No,' I say, feeling just like Luke Skywalker at the end of *The Empire Strikes Back*. 'And I wish you weren't my dad.'

THIS ISN'T THE FIRST TIME...

This isn't the first time that Dad's embarrassed me in front of everyone. I know most people think their parents are embarrassing, but my dad's literally the worst. For as long as I can remember, his incredibly weird behaviour has made me a laughing stock at school.

It all started on the first day of junior school. I remember how excited I was when I put on my new school uniform for the very first time, Mum proudly taking a picture of me with her mobile phone to send to my gran. Mum had an early shift on the ambulance, so Dad was the one who actually took me to school. I was feeling a bit nervous on the way there, worrying out loud whether I'd make any friends, but Dad told me I'd be fine. He said the best way to make new friends was to make people smile, but before I'd even got inside my classroom he'd made the whole school start screaming in terror.

It happened when I was lining up outside. All the parents had been kept on one side of the playground, whilst the teachers came out to collect their classes. My class were the first to start filing in, our teacher, Miss Hutchinson, leading the way, but when I turned round to wave goodbye to my dad, I saw that he'd turned green.

And when I say he'd turned green, I don't mean he looked like he was about to be sick. I mean, his skin was bright green – like he'd just been painted from head to toe with a tin of goblin-green paint. At first he didn't even seem to have noticed that he'd changed, blowing me a kiss as he waved goodbye. All the other kids in my class were waving to their parents too, but when the boy next to me spotted my dad, he shouted out, 'Monster!' and that's when it all kicked off.

Everyone started screaming at once. Kids were running in every direction, their parents sprinting across the playground to save them from the monster in their midst. Teachers were shouting, trying to get everyone to calm down, but nobody was listening. As far as the pupils of Oakwood Primary School were concerned, my dad was a big green monster who was going to eat them all for breakfast.

I remember standing there in the middle of the playground, tears rolling down my face whilst I tried to work out why Dad looked so strange.

It turned out to be an allergic reaction to the wheatgrass shake that he'd drunk for breakfast, the chlorophyll inside the drink turning my dad's skin bright green. That's what Mum told me, but the kids from school still reckoned my dad was some kind of monster. Some of them even started calling me 'Son of Shrek' and that's the nickname that's stuck for most of junior school.

I suppose I can't really blame my dad for an allergic reaction, but ever since then he always seems to find a new way to embarrass me.

Like on school sports day, when he took part in the dad's sack race and got himself disqualified for cheating. As soon as the whistle went to start the race, Dad started bouncing – his bounding leaps taking him the length of the track in six seconds flat, whilst the rest of the dads were still tangled up in their sacks near the start line. Dad bounced so far he actually ended up in the school car park, but by the time he got back to the field our head teacher had given first prize to Amba's dad instead. Mr Ronson reckoned my dad must've been hiding a pogo stick inside his sack to be able to jump like that and told him he should be ashamed of himself for cheating in front of the children. After that, I made sure I came last in the obstacle race. I didn't want anyone to think I was a cheat as well.

Then there was the time Dad joined the PTA and was put in charge of sorting out the toy stall for the summer fete. There was a huge pile of donations in the school hall and Dad was supposed to go through these to get rid of any broken toys and games. However, when I turned up with the rest of the Key Stage Two volunteers to bring out the trestle tables, we discovered my dad had spent the whole morning building a giant spaceship out of Lego.

It looked like some kind of intergalactic Kinder Surprise, the dome of the egg-shaped spaceship more than two metres tall. There must've been a million Lego bricks in that thing. I don't even know where Dad got them all from, let alone how he had time to build it in the time it took for the bouncy castle to inflate.

At first my friends were really impressed, but

when Dad tried to move his model spaceship outside, it started to roll out of control, taking out the soft drinks stall, the chocolate tombola and the second-hand uniform stand, before it bounced off the bouncy castle and exploded in a shower of Lego bricks. The St John Ambulance treated six teachers for minor injuries and then everyone blamed me when the summer fete was cancelled.

I thought this school concert was my chance to put all the teasing behind me at last. I never felt like I fitted in, but since I started at Gym Stars at least I feel like I'm good at something. I remember the 'ooohhs' and 'aaahhs' from the

audience as I raced through my routine, every twist, roll and somersault I made a perfect ten.

Then Dad had to jump on stage and ruin it all again.

i WANT A DiVORCe

I look down at my plate and see the message spelt out in lines of Alphabetti spaghetti across the toast.

JAKE
I AM SORRY
ABOUT THE SCHOOL CONCERT
CAN YOU FORGIVE ME
DAD

This isn't lunch – it's a letter of apology.

Dad sits down next to Mum at the kitchen table, his blue-green eyes glancing hopefully in my direction as he waits for my reply. When I say my dad has got blue-green eyes, that's exactly what I mean. His left eye is blue and his right eye is green. Just another thing that makes kids stop and stare and tell me my dad is seriously weird.

'Yum,' says Mum, picking up her knife and fork. 'My favourite. Again.'

She's joking, but I don't feel like laughing. And I don't feel like eating lunch any more either.

Getting up from the table, I push the plate away. 'I'm not hungry,' I say as I turn towards the door.

'Jake—' Dad begins, but I've slammed the door behind me before he can say another word.

I race up the stairs to my room, two steps at a time. I'm not talking to Dad. I haven't said a word to him since the school concert. My bedroom door is wide open so I slam this behind me too, letting the sound of my anger thud through the house.

I don't want to let this feeling go. The anger is like an energy inside me, but as I flop down on to my bed I just feel so tired of it all.

I remember the chants echoing round the hall, Dad waving in triumph to the audience whilst I was left dumped on my backside, sitting there forgotten on the floor.

There's a knock on my door.

I ignore it.

I'm still not talking to him.

Then the handle turns and Mum pops her head round the door.

'Jake,' she says. 'Are you OK?'

Sitting up on my bed, I shake my head.

'I want a divorce,' I tell her.

Mum laughs. 'What do you mean?' she asks. 'Jake, you're only ten years old. You've not even got a girlfriend yet, unless there's something you're not telling me.'

I blush. I haven't got a girlfriend. Well, I have got a friend who's a girl – Amba – but that's totally different and anyway that's not what I meant.

'I want a divorce from Dad,' I explain. 'I looked it up on the internet. It's a thing you can do. Divorce your parents. But I don't mean you. Just Dad.'

Mum's stopped laughing now. Quietly closing the door behind her, she sits down next to me on the bed. Brushing her dark fringe out of her eyes, Mum peers at me in concern.

'Surely things can't be that bad.'

I look at Mum in disbelief.

'Dad jumped on stage with a bin on his head and ruined my school concert. Everything he does is completely embarrassing and we're still eating Alphabetti spaghetti every day of the week.' I feel the anger inside me start to fizz again. 'How can you say things aren't that bad?'

Mum frowns, a worried look creasing the lines around her eyes. Her mouth opens then closes then opens again. It looks like she's about to say something, but can't seem to find the right words.

'Your dad's *different*, Jake,' she says finally. 'Yes, some of the things he does can seem a little odd, but he's got good hearts – I mean, heart. Just one.'

I look at Mum suspiciously. She's supposed to be the normal parent, but sometimes she sounds almost as strange as Dad.

'He knows he let you down last night,' Mum continues. 'He just got a bit overexcited when he saw you dressed up like Luke Skywalker. It reminded him of all those games you used to play together when you were younger. I used to watch the two of you in the back garden, fighting for hours with those toy lightsabers. Your dad just thought it would be fun to join in again. He didn't realize you'd be so angry with him.'

I want to stay angry at Dad, but as I close my eyes for a second the good memories come flooding back. I remember how we used to curl up on the sofa together with a bucket of popcorn for our *Star Wars* movie marathons. Then when the film ended we'd race out into the back garden for a lightsaber duel, Dad laughing as he tried to show me some Jedi Knight moves. And when it got dark we'd sit on the back step together, chatting as we stared at the stars. That's when Dad told me that one day he'd take me to a galaxy far, far away. He was joking, of course, but back then I used to think my dad could do anything.

Mum puts her arm around my shoulders as I open my eyes again.

'Give him the chance to show you that he's sorry, Jake,' she says, giving me a gentle hug. 'That's all your dad wants – the chance to make it up to you.'

I don't know what to say, so in the end I just nod my head.

ARE WE THERE YET?

'**A**re we there yet?'

'No.'

'Are we there yet?'

'No.'

'Are we there yet?'

'Dad, you're the one who's driving!' I finally snap, driven mad by his latest lame attempt to make me laugh. 'I don't even know where we're going.'

As the window wipers swish, I slump down in my car seat, unable to believe that I ever agreed to this trip in the first place. Mum said this weekend away would give me and Dad the perfect chance to reconnect, but when I tried to find out where we were going she told me it was a big surprise.

'Don't worry,' Mum said when she saw the worried look on my face. 'You're going to love it, Jake.'

So when we set off in the car this morning I kept my eyes fixed on the road signs to try and pick up some clues about our final destination. Maybe Dad was taking me to the theme park at the Pleasure Beach or perhaps he'd got us tickets for the big match. But when we turned off the main road to drive down this bumpy track through the trees, I started to get a bad feeling about this whole trip.

THUMP!

'Sorry,' Dad says, gripping the steering wheel tightly as the car bounces forward again. 'You used to think that joke was funny, Jake. But we are nearly there. Look!'

Up ahead, there's a brown sign pointing left with a picture of a tree and a tent.

THE GETAWAY EXPERIENCE
MIDDLEWICH FOREST
ACRES OF SPACE TO EXPLORE

'This is it!' Dad says as he swings the car left. 'What do you think?'

Parking up, Dad jumps out of the car and I have to follow him, shaking my head in horror at what I can see.

Surrounded by trees, I can see a massive field. But it's what's in this field that fills me with dread. I can see tents – tents of all shapes and sizes. Dome tents, cone-shaped tents, safari tents and tepees. There's even a huge tent that looks a flying saucer, slap bang in the middle of the field, its green canvas roof festooned with fairy lights.

'It's a campsite,' I say.

And I hate camping.

'No,' Dad says as my gaze roams across the field, looking for a way out. 'This isn't a campsite – this is a luxurious escape from the stresses of modern-day life. A place to build dens, climb trees and cook on a campfire under the stars. And from abseiling to zorbing, there's an A to Z of adventure to be found at the Getaway Experience.'

I glance across at him suspiciously. 'Are you reading this off a leaflet?'

'No,' Dad says, quickly tucking his hands behind his back.

Raising an eyebrow, I hold my hand out. 'Let me see.'

Reluctantly, like he's been caught cheating, Dad pulls a leaflet out from behind his back.

'OK, maybe I was a little,' he admits. 'But take a look, Jake. This place sounds amazing.'

Located in the beautiful woodland of Middlewich Forest, the Getaway Experience puts the 'glam' into camping! Our stylish tents and lodges provide a cosy home from home with luxurious beds, log burners, en-suite bathrooms and free Wi-Fi.

I glance up from the leaflet, now seeing the tents in a new light as the sun finally comes out. Maybe Dad's right. If it's got free Wi-Fi, this place might be OK after all.

'So which is our tent then?' I ask as Dad lifts the car boot open. 'I hope I get my own room.'

'Erm, not exactly,' Dad replies as he rummages around in the boot. 'I'm afraid all the on-site tents and caravans were fully booked, but I've pulled a few strings and managed to find a place we can stay.'

He pulls a black canvas bag out of the boot. It's flat and round and I can see the words POP-UP TENT written on the side. Dad grins as he tosses this to me.

'This is going to be so much more fun.'

WORST TRIP EVER

'Tent assemble!'

I'm standing in the pouring rain, listening to the sound of Dad arguing with the tent pegs. The bright yellow fabric of the flysheet flaps in the wind – our only chance of staying dry tonight is in danger of flying away.

Dad always does this when things don't work – starts talking at stuff like he thinks it's going to listen to him. The instructions said this pop-up tent would only take two seconds to assemble. *Open bag, unpack and watch your smart tent spring to life!* But whoever wrote the instructions hadn't met my dad. When he tipped the bag open, the tent just seemed to fall to pieces and Dad's spent the last ten minutes shouting at the bits. I don't think he realizes this smart tent isn't voice-activated.

'It's no use,' Dad says, scrambling to hold on to the canvas. 'It looks like we're going to have to assemble this ourselves. Grab hold of that pole, Jake.'

I look down at the tangle of poles, ropes and pegs scattered on the ground.

'Which one?'

'That one,' Dad says, letting go of the flysheet for a moment to point down at one of the poles.

Bad idea.

In an instant, the bright yellow canvas is whipped away by the wind.

'I'll get it!' I shout, scrambling to grab hold of the flysheet as it flaps just out of reach. Behind me, I hear Dad groan in despair.

We started to pitch our tent at the very edge of the field, out of sight of all the fancy tents and caravans. But as the wind gusts again, its bright yellow fabric is whirled away into the trees. I chase after it, dodging past branches as I dive into the woods.

'Wait for me!' Dad shouts.

For a second, the flysheet snags on a tree branch, but as I reach out to grab it the wind whips the tent away again. It soars upwards and onwards, out of sight, and my heart sinks into my squelching trainers.

I trudge on through the gloom of the forest. Trees, trees and more boring trees – this is turning into the worst trip ever. At least it isn't raining any more under the cover of the leaves and maybe, if the tent's gone missing, we can just get back in the car and go home.

Then I spot a flash of yellow in a gap through the trees. Hurrying forward, the trees start to open out and I see the flysheet in the middle of a clearing. The wind's died down now, leaving the bright yellow canvas draped in a tent-like shape. At first I think that the tent must have popped itself up at last, but as the canvas gently flaps I catch a glimpse of something metallic underneath. It looks like it's caught on something.

Reaching the centre of the clearing, I pull back the flysheet and then gasp in surprise as I see what's underneath.

It's a UFO.

A flying saucer.

Actually, it looks more like an intergalactic iron – the black metallic form of the spaceship curving in a triangular shape. And where the handle should be, there's a dome-like cockpit instead, made out of the same impenetrable black metal.

Then I see the notice fixed to the side of this spaceship and breathe out a sigh of relief.

PLEASE DO NOT CLIMB, SIT ON OR DEFACE THE UFO
SCULPTURE. THIS IS A WORK OF ART.

Still holding the bright yellow flysheet, I take a step back, trying to work out why anyone has left a sculpture of a flying saucer in the middle of the woods. Looking around I spot a post with an arrow pointing the way to the trail but, before I can investigate this, I hear the sound of my dad calling from the trees.

'Jake!'

I turn round to see him enter the clearing. With a shocked expression on his face, Dad looks from the flysheet to the flying saucer and then back again. Beneath the shade of the leaves, it almost looks like he's turning green . . .

'Don't worry,' I quickly say, worried that he's about to be sick. 'It's just a sculpture – not some kind of alien invader.'

'I knew that,' Dad replies defensively, the green tinge slowly fading from his cheeks. 'I was just a bit surprised, that's all. Not that there's anything wrong with an alien invader . . .'

Dad's voice trails into silence as he stares at the sculpture, his blue-green gaze glinting with a faraway look. He opens his mouth as if he's about to say something else, but then the eerie sound of a siren suddenly echoes through the trees.

'Come on,' Dad says with a shake of his head, grabbing hold of the flysheet and motioning for me to follow him. 'It's starting.'

WELCOME, DADVENTURERS!

On the bright side, the sound of the siren wasn't announcing a visit from the intergalactic emergency services.

It's much, much worse than that.

'Welcome, Dadventurers!'

Brandishing the crimson-red klaxon that has brought us all here, the outdoor instructor greets us with a fresh-faced smile.

'And welcome, Kidsplorers too. My name's Flip Foxley and I'm here to show you the ropes on this *Dads and Kids' Adventure Weekend*.'

Sitting down next to my dad, I sneak a look

at the rest of the campers now gathered on the wooden benches under the roof of this giant tent. When Mum said we'd get some father-son bonding time on this trip, I didn't think it was going to be with a load of other dads and kids too. There are tall dads, short dads, bald

dads and bearded dads, each one sitting in a pair with their own 'kidsplorer'. I recognize some of my friends from school, Amba giving me a sneaky wave whilst her dad's gaze stays fixed on his mobile phone. Damon's here too, his dad nudging him to attention as Flip Foxley continues to speak.

'Now, modern life can be filled with distractions: smartphones, games consoles, TV box sets and viral videos,' Flip says, his confident manner daring anyone to disagree. 'But here at the Getaway Experience, you'll put all these distractions to one side and focus instead on making memories that will last a lifetime.'

With a click of his fingers, Flip holds out his hand for Amba's dad's phone.

Mr Flixton hands this over with a grumbling apology. 'Sorry, I was just checking my work email.'

'All work and no play makes for a dull dad,' Flip says with a cheeky grin as he pockets the mobile phone. He turns towards Amba and fires a question straight at her. 'Do you want a dad who checks emails or climbs trees?'

'Climbs trees!' Amba grins.

'And is your dad snoring boring?' Flip asks, spinning round to face Damon. 'Or is he brave enough to go zorbing?'

'Zorbing!' Damon shouts.

Flip dances round the yurt, firing out his questions like a laser blaster. Build a campfire or fix the boiler? Sleep under the stars or clean the car? Every question he asks sends the excitement levels rising even higher until Flip's standing right in front of me.

'And how about you?' he asks, doing a sudden double-take as he glances across at my dad. 'Do you want an ordinary dad or a dad who's out of this world?'

I shake my head as I turn to look at the embarrassment sitting next to me. Everybody else's dad is wearing a sensible fleece or a waterproof jacket – the perfect gear for a camping weekend – but my dad seems to be dressed in a spacesuit. Well, it's not exactly a spacesuit, but a one-piece ski suit made out of the same shiny silver material. Dad says this reflects the heat inside, keeping him toasty and warm. I think it makes him look like a jacket potato. The shiny foil rustles as Dad turns towards me with a hopeful smile.

I just want an ordinary dad, but how can I say this now?

'Out of this world,' I finally sigh.

'OK then,' Flip grins as he claps his hands together. 'It's time for some close encounters of the fun kind. Dadventurers and Kidsplorers, it's time to reach for the stars.'

GRAVITY ISN'T ANYTHING TO BE SCARED OF

I don't dare look down as I stand on the swaying platform.

Flip said this was going to be fun, but as I cling to a rope dangling from a metal hook that's holding me twenty-five metres above the forest floor, fun's the last thing I'm thinking of. I shuffle forward to the edge of the platform, the harness that's keeping me safe digging into some particularly uncomfortable places.

Ahead of me I can see the obstacles that

are slung between the treetops: narrow beams and swaying rope bridges, tightrope walks and Tarzan swings. A large rope net is stretched between the tallest of the trees, like some giant spider's web, and above this I glimpse the final platform that leads to the double zip wire down.

It didn't look this high when we were on the ground.

That's where Flip showed us the ropes, training us how to use the safety cables and pulleys that attach to our harnesses, each one colour-coded so we know exactly where to clip them. It all seemed so easy down there, but that was before I climbed the rope ladder that led up to this obstacle course in the sky. My hands shake as I unclip the carabiner, the metal hook clacking as I hook it to the red safety line that's stretched alongside the obstacles.

'Come on, Jake,' Amba calls out from across the abyss. 'You can do it!'

All the others are already back down on the ground. I've watched them wobbling across the obstacles, two by two, each dad and kid taking it in turns to lead the way, just like Flip showed us to. Now there's just Dad and me left on this first wooden platform and I don't think I can go any further.

I hear the outdoor instructor's voice float up from the forest floor.

'Now for the last two,' he shouts. 'Take it easy, guys, and you'll beat the treetop challenge in no time.'

At the sound of this shout, I make the mistake of glancing down and feel my stomach flip. The ground seems to swim into view and I glimpse the outdoor instructor's upturned face staring up at me from so far away. I freeze, my fingers tightening around the safety line. We're even higher than I thought.

Then Dad taps me on the shoulder, the shock of this almost launching me off the edge.

'Are you ready?'

I shake my head, fear thumping in my chest as I slowly back away from the edge.

'I – I can't do it.'

Standing next to me, Dad looks surprised, the lines around his blue-green eyes creasing in concern.

'What's the matter, Jake?' he asks, and his gaze flicks from my face to the obstacle course ahead. He gives a tug on the safety line, making my stomach lurch. 'You don't need to worry. It's completely safe.'

I shake my head again, barely able to get my words out in reply.

'It's . . . too . . . high,' I stutter. 'What if I fall?'

Dad rests his arm on my shoulder, the gently reassuring weight of this helping me to take a breath.

'The only reason things fall is because of gravity,' Dad explains, plucking a leaf from an overhanging branch and letting this flutter to the ground. 'And gravity isn't anything to be scared of. It's just the bending of space and time. It can help you to speed up or slow down and even change direction. And if you use it cleverly, it can even make it seem like you can fly.'

Lifting his arm from my shoulder, Dad clips his carabiner on to the safety line ahead of mine.

'Watch.'

Then my heart leaps in my chest as Dad takes a flying leap from the edge of the platform.

'Dad!'

The safety line whirrs as Dad lands in the middle of the narrow beam, his darting footsteps catapulting him forward so it looks like he's skimming the trees. Everyone else took ages to cross this first obstacle, but my dad's cleared it in seconds flat.

Using his momentum, he swings round the platform that rings the next tree trunk, launching himself on to the swaying rope bridge that climbs to the next. I hear the shocked gasps coming from those watching down below as Dad uses this to bounce even higher. His springing steps make it look like he's dancing in mid-air.

'Come on, Jake!' he shouts over his shoulder. 'It's just like gymnastics.'

With a beckoning wave to encourage me on, Dad grabs hold of the Tarzan swing at the end of the rope bridge and then jumps into the unknown. I watch open-mouthed as he soars through the empty air. For a second it looks like he *is* flying, his hands letting go of the swing as it reaches the crest of its arc. Gravity takes him the rest of the way – a relieved cheer erupting from all those down below as Dad lands safely in the middle of the cargo net that's stretched between the trees.

He made it look easy, but as Dad scrambles up the rope net to reach the zip wire at the top, I still don't know if I can follow him.

My throat feels dry as I pace out the obstacles in my mind. Gravity isn't anything to be scared of, Dad said. It's just like gymnastics.

And that's one thing I'm good at.

Carefully checking that the metal loop of my carabiner is still fastened to the red safety line, I take a deep breath and then launch myself straight off the edge.

For a second I'm flying, then I feel the safety line tugging me back as I land slap bang on the spot I was aiming for – right in the middle of the beam. It's slippery from the rain but, as my feet adjust to keep my balance, I realize that it's actually three times as wide as the beam I practise on at Gym Stars. And this means I can really show off some of my tricks.

Adrenalin racing, I launch myself forward in a tumbling run, somersaulting head over heels as I soar through the treetops. I can hear the whirr of the safety line ringing in my ear as I reach the end of the beam. I'm not looking down, my gaze still firmly fixed on the obstacles ahead.

Following Dad's lead, I swing round the platform and land with a boing on the bouncing rope bridge. Trampolining forward, I can hear the others 'oohing' and 'aahing' as each bounce takes me higher still. Dad was right. Gravity's just the bending of space and time and, as I twist to grab hold of the Tarzan swing, it's making me feel like I can do anything.

'Go on, Jake!' Amba calls out from the ground below.

With a grin, I swing out across the abyss, the rope net racing up to meet me as I grasp hold of the webbing. Everyone's cheering me on as I scramble to the top.

Dad's waiting for me there, holding out his hand to help me up as I clamber on to the final platform.

'Well done, Jake,' he says, greeting me with a grin. 'I knew you could do it.'

Dad still looks ridiculous in his silver ski suit, but I can't stop myself from grinning back at him.

'Ready for the final challenge?' he asks.

I nod my head.

'You bet,' I reply. 'All we've got left now is the easy part.'

It's time to fly.

Looping myself on to the zip wire, I look at the ground below. It's a long way down, but somehow I don't feel scared any more. Dad showed me the way to beat my fear and, as he loops himself on to the zip wire parallel to mine, I start to think that maybe this weekend was a good idea after all.

'On the count of three,' Dad says, the two of

us holding on to our zip wire straps as we stand on the platform edge. '*One, two, wheeeeeeeeee!*'

Gravity whips his words away as I step into thin air and feel myself fall. The cable buzzes with a quickening whine as I hurtle through the trees. I feel my skin tingling with excitement as I fly through the air, the world rushing towards me at what feels like super-speed. I can't stop myself from joining in with Dad's whoops of triumph as we race towards the landing site. I can see the rest of the dads and kids waiting for us there, everyone clapping wildly as the zip

wire brakes kick in and we hit the ground in a shower of wood chips.

I can't stop myself from smiling as I pick myself up off the ground. My skin is still tingling as I turn towards my dad with a grin, but then I see the look of surprise on his face as the clapping quickly fades away.

I look around.

Everyone is staring at me. Flip Foxley has turned as white as a sheet, whilst Damon and Amba just look really worried.

'What's the matter?' I ask, brushing the wood chips from my clothes. Then I catch a glimpse of my hands and stare at them in surprise.

They seem to have turned bright green.

THE MIDDLEWICH INCIDENT

It wasn't just my hands that turned green, but the skin on my face too. That's why everyone was staring at me. At first I panicked, thinking I was turning into the Incredible Hulk, but Dad managed to calm me down. He told everyone I was having an allergic reaction. He reckoned the broccoli and stilton cup-a-soup that we'd had for lunch must've turned my skin a bright shade of green. Dad says I must be chlorophyll-intolerant, just like him.

My skin's turned back to normal now. It

only lasted for a few minutes, but I'm never eating broccoli again. So that's a positive, I suppose.

The negative is all the jokes about little green men I've had to listen to as we gather round this flying saucer that's still parked in the middle of the woods. Flip has brought us here for the final challenge of the day, the sun setting behind the trees casting a strange golden glow across the fake spaceship.

'Don't worry,' Flip says as Amba pokes it with a pointy stick. 'This flying saucer is just a sculpture. It marks the spot where a UFO was spotted here in Middlewich Forest, twelve years ago.'

One of the dads starts humming under his breath.

Doo-doo-DOO-doo, doo-doo-DOO-doo.

Flip just ignores this.

'Was it aliens?' Amba asks, keeping a tight grip on her stick.

'Some people say it was just a shooting star,'

Flip replies mysteriously as the darkness in the forest grows. 'Several eyewitnesses saw strange glowing spheres falling into the forest that evening but when the police went to investigate, all they found was a trail of phosphorescent footsteps leading from this clearing.'

Flip pauses, a spooky silence hanging over the woods as night creeps across the sky.

'As the police followed the glowing trail, one of the officers claimed that she glimpsed the figure of a spaceman running through the trees. When she shouted for him to stop, the figure just vanished into thin air but, before he disappeared, the policewoman says she caught a glimpse of an alien face.'

As the shadows lengthen, Flip turns his gaze in my direction.

'She says that it looked bright green.'

Some people start to giggle, thinking that Flip is making fun of me. I feel myself start to blush. I wish I hadn't drunk that cup-a-soup . . .

'So for your final challenge this evening,'

Flip continues, ignoring the giggles as Dad shuffles his feet next to me. 'I'm going to send you on an alien hunt.'

A sudden flash of light makes everyone jump.

'Sorry,' Dad says as he waves his torch around. 'Actually, don't you think it's getting rather dark? I'm not sure any kind of alien hunt is a good idea right now. There are a lot of trip hazards out there in the woods.'

'And that's why I gave you these torches,' Flip replies, raising his hand to block out the torchlight's glare. 'Don't worry, Mr Jones, the only danger you'll face on this alien hunt is the possibility of missing out on a campfire treat.'

Flip gestures in the direction of the main campsite.

'I've hidden some unidentified flying goodies on the trail through the trees. Bring any you find back to the yurt and we'll have a feast there under the stars.'

Everyone else lights up their torches, the

flashing beams showing which way to go.

'Remember to keep your eyes peeled,' Flip calls out, as we set off down the path. 'The treasure is out there somewhere.'

Dad tries to put his arm around my shoulder, but I quickly shake it off.

'I'm going to walk with my friends,' I say, hurrying to catch up with Damon and Amba. The rest of the Dadventurers and Kidsplorers are already racing ahead, everyone eager to be first to find any extraterrestrial treats.

'Hey, Jake,' Amba says as I fall into step beside them. 'Are you feeling better now?'

'I'm fine,' I say. 'It was just some stupid allergy.'

'It didn't stop you showing off your Gym Star skills,' she grins. 'I thought you were going to end up in orbit when you started somersaulting across that obstacle course. Weren't you scared?'

'I was a bit at first,' I reply, glancing back over my shoulder as Dad hangs back in a sulk.

'But I couldn't let my dad leave me in the shade again. Not after the school concert.'

'It was out of this world,' Amba says. 'It almost looked like the two of you were flying.'

I grin, but before I can say anything else Damon chips in. 'Do you think Flip was making up that story about a spaceman landing in the woods?' he says, peering nervously into the trees. 'Aliens don't exist, do they?'

'What about Roswell?' Amba replies, flipping her torch up so it rests beneath her chin. The bright-white beam gives her face an unearthly glow. 'A UFO crash-landed there years ago. Apparently they captured the aliens and took them to a top-secret military base at Area 51 to dissect them. Maybe the alien who landed here was a friend of theirs and came looking for revenge.'

'Stop it, Amba,' Damon scowls. 'You're spooking me out.'

Up ahead, the trail starts to twist and I watch the waving torch beams of the others slowly disappear from view. It's getting darker and, as I glance up into the night sky, I see the stars are starting to come out. I think about the campfire feast that Flip has promised us and my stomach starts to rumble. That broccoli and stilton cup-a-soup now seems a long time ago.

'Come on,' I say. 'We need to catch them up.'

'Wait a second,' Amba says, stopping dead in her tracks. 'What's that?'

At first I think Amba's joking, still trying to give Damon a fright. But when I look through the trees in the direction that she's pointing, I see a faint orange glow, almost hidden by the undergrowth.

The others must have missed this.

'It must be an unidentified flying goodie,' I grin. 'An alien treat and I'm going to get it.'

Taking care not to slip, I head off the path in the direction of the light.

'Be careful,' Damon shouts.

The ground is muddy underfoot, soggy

puddles hiding beneath the branches as I pick my way through the trees. The eerie glow gets brighter as I peel back the leaves, revealing a luminous Sainsbury's bag that's been left hanging from a low branch.

'What is it?' Amba calls out.

Reaching up to unhook the glowing bag, I open it up to take a look inside. I just hope it's not a radioactive dog poo.

It isn't.

The shining glow is coming from a bicycle lamp that's been left inside along with an intergalactic surprise.

FUN-SIZE FLYING SAUCER MARSHMALLOWS, the packet says, a picture of a friendly green alien staring out of the front. THEY TASTE OUT OF THIS WORLD!

'It's definitely alien,' I shout, reaching inside the bag to grab hold of the party pack of marshmallows.

And that's when Dad comes running through the trees.

'Get down, Jake!' he shouts, pushing me to one side as he rips the glowing bag from my hands. I feel the packet split as it's torn from my fingers, flying saucers soaring through the air as I slip and land face down in the mud.

SPLAT!

Spluttering in surprise, I lift my head to see a fleet of marshmallow spaceships floating in front of me in the muddy puddle. I'm soaking wet, slime clinging to my clothes as I scramble to my feet.

'You – you *pushed* me!'

Dad shakes his head grimly as he keeps his gaze fixed on the glowing bag in his hand.

'I saved you, Jake,' he says, his silvery ski suit shimmering in the unearthly light. 'Inside this bag is a piece of alien technology that could turn you into a pile of smouldering atoms.'

Cautiously reaching inside the bag, he pulls out the bicycle lamp. Its shining beam illuminates the look of surprise now spreading across Dad's face.

'Oh.'

His gaze swivels towards me, realization slowly dawning as he sees the mud-splattered marshmallows scattered around my feet. My clothes drip soggily on to this feast of flying saucers as my anger quickly grows.

'Oh no.'

i JUST WANT TO GO HOME

I squat inside the pop-up tent, stuffing my ruined clothes into a rucksack. Dad's not back yet and in the distance I can hear the rest of them laughing around the campfire.

Laughing at me.

Shaking my head, I pull the drawstring of my rucksack tight. I've packed all my stuff and now I just want to go home.

It was bad enough being pushed into the mud, but what made it worse was Damon and Amba's reaction. At first my friends looked so worried when they raced to my side, but then, as their gazes flicked from my dad to me and back again, Amba couldn't stop herself from giggling.

'What's so funny?' I snapped as the slime dripped down my face.

'I'm sorry, Jake,' Amba replied as Damon tried to hide his smile. 'But you should see the both of you. Your dad looks like he's just stepped out of a spaceship while you look like a swamp monster from Mars. Don't let Flip catch you like this or he'll think the aliens really have landed this time.'

Crawling out through the tent flap, I stare up into the darkness of the sky. The stars look so much brighter than I've ever seen them before, but right now I feel so alone. Mum said this trip would give Dad the chance to make things right, but he's just made it all go wrong.

I smell my dad before I see him, the sickly-sweet scent of toasted marshmallows following him on the breeze as he walks up the field.

'I thought you were coming down to the campfire once you got yourself changed? Don't worry, I've told Flip to save some marshmallows for you,' he calls out cheerily.

As he reaches the tent, Dad looks down at the rucksack on the ground beside me.

'What's the matter, Jake? Are you feeling OK?'

I shake my head, remembering the flying saucer marshmallows floating in front of my face as I pulled my head out of the muddy puddle.

'No,' I say, fighting to keep a lid on my anger. 'I'm not OK. Now just leave me alone.'

Dad ignores me, moving my rucksack to one side as he sits down on the grass. I shuffle along on my bottom as I try to move away, but it's not the smell of burnt marshmallows that's making me feel sick.

'Come on, Jake,' Dad begins. 'Don't be like this. You'll feel different when you've had something to eat. Let's go down to the campfire together. Flip said I can borrow his acoustic guitar.'

The thought of Dad leading a campfire singalong pushes me over the edge and I can't stop myself from snapping out loud, 'I *said*, go away! Why would I want to come down to the campfire when everyone's laughing at me? You've ruined everything, Dad, and I just want to go home.'

I can't even look at him, keeping my gaze fixed on the stars as I blink back my tears.

A long silence fills the space between us, but Dad stays where he is.

'I'm sorry, Jake,' he says finally. 'I know I made a mistake, but I was just trying to protect you back there. I thought you were in danger. I thought we both were.'

'You were just playing a stupid game! Blabbering on about alien technology when I'd already found the marshmallow flying saucers.' I turn towards Dad, his ridiculous ski suit shining silver in the moonlight. 'Why did you even bring me here if you were just going to embarrass me again?'

Dad shakes his head. 'I never meant to embarrass you, Jake. And I wasn't playing a game. There's something that you need to know. Something I've been meaning to tell you for a very long time.'

Dad usually acts like everything's a joke, but right now he looks so serious.

'I brought you here because this is where it all began. Sort of.'

i don't believe in aliens

'**W**hat do you mean, "this is where it all began"?' I ask, still feeling angry as I glance around the campsite. 'Have you been here before?'

Dad looks up into the starry sky and sighs.

'Only for a flying visit,' he replies. 'And it was a long time ago. Twelve years, to be precise.'

It takes a second or two for this to sink in.

'Wait a minute. Flip said that was when the UFO was spotted here. Are you trying to tell me you saw the alien too?'

Dad shakes his head. 'I didn't *see* the alien. I *was* the alien.'

I can't stop myself from laughing out loud.

'Don't be stupid,' I say, staring at my dad in disbelief. 'You can't be an alien – you're from Wales.'

His blue-green eyes seem to sparkle in the silvery light.

'I'm not actually from Wales, Jake. That's just something I had to put on my passport application. I come from a planet that orbits a star four light years away from Earth.'

'Yeah, right,' I reply as I wait for the punchline to this latest Dad joke. 'So what's this planet called then? Tattooine? Gallifrey? Krypton?'

Dad takes a deep breath and then makes a noise that sounds like a cow driving a motorbike full speed through an electric fence.

'Mmbogbjsqxmmhxzohzmmhphfszdixzs oespcxmmmmbouztjmjphphphpdi.'

As this strange sound splutters to a finish, Dad pauses to wipe his mouth with the back of his sleeve.

'But the astronomers on this planet call it Proxima b.'

I wait for him to crack a smile to show me that he's joking. But the expression on Dad's face doesn't change. He looks really serious. Like he believes that it's true.

I shake my head. 'I don't believe in aliens.'

In reply, Dad points towards the night sky. 'How many stars can you see, Jake?'

I look up into the darkness and see the stars shining brightly there. I start to try and count them, but quickly give up.

'I don't know,' I say. 'There's too many to count.'

'Take a look here,' Dad says, his finger tracing a silvery trail of stars as they spill across the sky. 'This is the Milky Way – the galaxy that we live in. And it contains more than one hundred billion stars.'

His finger drifts across the darkness until it's pointing to a blurry point of light, just above the trees.

'And do you know what this is?' he asks.

'Another star, I guess.'

Dad shakes his head. 'This is Andromeda – a whole other galaxy, twice as big as the Milky Way. In this tiny point of light there are more than two hundred billion stars. And the universe contains trillions of galaxies, each one with hundreds of billions of stars. All those stars have planets spinning round them, billions just like this one. All a planet needs for life to exist is an atmosphere, some organic compounds and a dash of liquid water. And sometimes not even that. So do you really think that out of all those billions of planets, Earth is the only place where intelligent life has evolved?'

Dad gently rests his arm around my shoulder.

'The universe is a very big place, Jake, and it's teeming with aliens.'

Dropping my gaze from the stars, I turn to look at my dad. He still looks deadly serious. It's time for me try another tactic to get him to drop this crazy idea.

'OK,' I say. 'Pretend that I believe you. If there are really all these aliens flying around up there, why haven't we seen them yet?'

'Because Earth has been placed in a Cosmic Zone of Exclusion.'

'A Cosmic Zone of What?'

'Exclusion,' Dad replies. 'This means the Earth is shut off from the rest of the universe. All P-class planets are placed in one.'

'P-class planets?'

'Primitive worlds,' Dad replies. 'Places where intelligent life exists, but only in a primitive form. Like planet Earth.'

I stare at my dad, dumbfounded.

'The human race isn't primitive!'

'I know that, Jake,' Dad replies, holding his hands up in apology. 'But I'm afraid this isn't the impression the human race has given to the universe. The Cosmic Authority spotted there was intelligent life on this planet eighty years ago when they detected radio and television signals leaking from Earth's atmosphere and escaping into interstellar space. At first the universe celebrated, eager to welcome a new member to the cosmic family of intelligent civilizations. But then they started to watch and listen to the signals that this planet was sending . . .'

Dad's sentence trails off into a pained silence.

'What do you mean?' I ask, still convinced that my dad has completely lost the plot. 'Did they start watching *The X-Factor* and realize we couldn't sing?'

Dad shakes his head.

'No,' he replies, 'I don't think *The X-Factor* was on eighty years ago. The signals the Cosmic Authority detected brought them the news and they were horrified by what they saw and heard. Reports of fighting and famine, wars and global warming – a planet plagued with selfishness, aggression and greed. Life on Earth was judged to be truly primitive and a decision was made to forbid any advanced alien civilization from making contact with this planet. If the human race couldn't care for its own world, imagine how it would treat the rest of the universe.'

My mouth gapes wide in disbelief as Dad continues to speak, every word he says a fresh type of crazy.

'A sphere of silence was placed around this solar system to prevent any of the primitive ideas the Earth was infected with from spreading across the universe. All TV and radio signals were blocked and any attempts to communicate with humanity or travel to this planet strictly forbidden by order of the Cosmic Authority.'

Dad's totally lost the plot, but I suddenly see a way to prove he's making all this up.

'But if aliens aren't allowed to come to planet Earth, how can *you* be one then?'

'Well, I've never been too good at following the rules,' Dad replies with a cheeky smile. 'And when my spaceship picked up a stray signal from Earth, I just had to come and take a look.'

'What kind of signal?'

'The radio waves came through on my translation circuits,' Dad explains, glancing up at the sky with a faraway look in his eyes. 'At first I thought it was a distress call from someone who was lost in space. The loneliest voice I'd ever heard telling me he was sitting in a tin can, far above a blue planet. His circuit was dead and there was nothing he could do. I had to try and help him. Turning my spaceship round, I headed straight for the source of the signal: planet Earth.'

Dad's words sound strangely familiar and it's only as he carries on talking that I realize why.

'But when I reached this solar system, the distress call just faded into silence. And when I found the blue planet that he'd told me about, there was no sign of Major Tom anywhere.'

The words of Dad's favourite song click together in my head. 'Space Oddity'.

'Wait a second,' I say. 'Are you trying to tell me you came to Earth because you heard a song by David Bowie?'

Dad nods his head. 'I didn't realize this at first. I didn't even know what a song was back then. But as I got closer to Earth I realized the whole planet was singing. All the signals that the sphere of silence had blocked from reaching interstellar space now rang out loud and clear. I could hear the sounds on my translation circuits: strange instruments and twinkling voices calling across the loneliness of space.'

His foot taps in time as he looks at the stars. 'I knew it was strictly forbidden to visit a P-class planet, but since I was already in the neighbourhood I didn't think it would do any harm to take a closer look. But as soon as I entered Earth's orbit, everything went wrong.'

His gaze traces an arc across the sky as if reliving the memory.

'The Cosmic Authority had set a guard around this planet and I came under attack. My spaceship was chased as I spiralled out of control. All my systems were dead, and my only chance of escape before my craft was destroyed was an emergency teleport to the surface of this strange alien world. I was still being hunted and had to run for my life. That's what the police officer who Flip told us about must've seen twelve years ago – the moment I fell to Earth.'

Lowering his gaze, Dad looks deeply into my eyes.

'I'm telling you the truth, Jake.'

I stare at my dad, but if feels like I'm looking

at him through the wrong end of a telescope. He seems so much smaller than he should be – like I'm the grown-up and he's the little kid making up this crazy story about flying saucers, aliens and a space oddity. But how can I make him stop?

The words come out of my mouth before I have the chance to think about what might happen next.

'Prove it.'

LiGHTSABERS ARE
KiND OF LAME

'Prove what?' Dad asks as the sound of an acoustic guitar and a chorus of 'Kumbaya' drifts across from the campfire.

'Prove that you're an alien,' I tell him, the two of us standing beneath the stars. The shadows of the trees at the forest's edge stretch towards us like trailing tentacles. 'In the movies, every alien who comes to Earth has got some kind of special ability. Superman can fly, Skrulls are shape-shifters and E.T. can use his finger like a torch. What extraterrestrial powers have you got, Dad?'

'Errrr,' Dad scratches his head as he ponders the question. 'I don't think I have got any special abilities.'

He waggles the tip of his finger, but this doesn't light up.

'You see, my home planet is a lot like Earth. It's got the same kind of atmosphere, land and liquid water - even the weather's pretty much the same, although Manchester gets a bit more rain. The only thing that's really different is the gravity.'

'What do you mean?'

'Well, the gravity here on Earth is a little lower than I'm used to,' Dad explains. 'So sometimes this makes me *feel* like I can fly. That's what I was trying to tell you when we were tackling the treetop challenge.'

I remember Dad dancing across the swaying rope bridge, my heart in my mouth as I watched him soar through the air.

'That doesn't prove anything,' I say. 'You're just good at gymnastics – exactly like me. Mrs Mays always says it's like I forget gravity exists when I get on the gymnastics mat, but that doesn't mean I'm an alien.'

'OK,' Dad replies. 'But what about the fact that your skin turned bright green?'

'That was an allergic reaction!' I explode. It was bad enough listening to everyone else's jokes about little green men without my dad joining in. 'I don't know why you're making up this stupid story, but I don't want to play your silly games any more.'

Angrily, I start to turn away, but Dad reaches out a hand to stop me.

'I'm not making it up, Jake. I can prove what I'm saying is true.' He reaches into his pocket. 'I can show you some real alien technology.'

'What is it?' I ask, unable to hide my sarcasm. 'A lightsaber? We're not playing games in the garden, Dad.'

Dad shakes his head. 'Lightsabers are kind

of lame, Jake,' he replies, opening up his hand to show me what he's got there. 'This is much more powerful.'

A small, egg-shaped stone, jet-black in colour, sits in the centre of his palm.

I stare at this, open-mouthed. 'It's a pebble.'

'No, no, no,' Dad replies. 'This is the Quintessence – the beating heart of my spaceship. And since my spaceship was vaporized, it's the only alien technology I've got left.'

Picking up the pebble, he twists this between his fingers and I gasp in surprise as starry lights suddenly shimmer across the surface of the stone.

'With its emergency settings activated, the Quintessence is equipped with a universal translator, harmonic modulating circuit, cloaking shield and quantum flare. This device saved my life when I landed here on Earth.'

Dad's words don't make any sense to me, but I can't tear my eyes away from the glittering pebble.

'How?' I ask as Dad places it in the palm of my hand.

'I was being hunted by killer robots, searching for any sign of rogue alien life. The only way to escape was to go undercover – as a human being. The harmonic modulating circuit reprogrammed my biology, whilst the cloaking shield disguised any trace of alien technology. I used the universal translator to help me pick up the local lingo and then my transformation was complete. Goodbye, Ion of Mmbogbjsqxmmhxzohzmmhphfszdixzsoespcxmmmmmbouztjmjphphphpdi. Hello, Ion Jones.'

Using the back of my sleeve, I wipe the spittle from my face.

'Can't you just call it planet Mmbog?'

'You can call it what you like,' Dad replies in a wistful tone, his gaze drifting upwards towards the night sky. 'With my spaceship gone, I'm never going back there. The only way off this planet is if I activated the quantum flare – and I wouldn't be stupid enough to do that.'

I turn the pebble over in my hand. Flickering lights ripple across its surface as I look for the place where the batteries go. I still can't really believe what he's telling me. This must be a toy, not some piece of alien technology. Copying my dad, I twist the egg-shaped pebble between my fingers and grin as I feel it catch with a click.

Then the lights go out.

Not just on the Quintessence, but everywhere.

The fairy lights strewn over the roof of the yurt, the lanterns hanging across the campsite, even the neon signs outside the toilet block. Everything's dark and I hear my dad groan as I turn my gaze to the stars.

They're not there. The sky is completely black, as though someone has thrown a cloak across the universe, hiding every star from view. My head spins as I stare up into the infinite darkness.

Panicking, I twist the device again and the stars come back out with a click.

I look around the campsite, the fairy lights and lanterns shine brightly once more as the singalong splutters to a stop.

'What – what just happened?'

Dad snatches the Quintessence off me, its flickering lights now pulsing with a strange red glow.

'You activated the quantum flare!'

As Dad speaks, the night air seems to prickle with a strange electricity. It feels like a storm is brewing.

'What do you mean?' I ask.

'Inside the Quintessence is an emergency distress signal – a quantum flare – that when activated instantly communicates its location across the universe. They'll know we're here!'

Dad frantically shakes the pebble, trying to turn it off somehow.

And that's when I see the glowing spheres of light, drifting slowly down out of the dark sky. The hairs on the back of my neck stand on end.

'Is that ball lightning?' I ask, pointing up towards the strange blue-white orbs. They seem to be growing brighter as they descend and I hear the others shouting in surprise.

'That's not lightning,' Dad replies, grabbing hold of my arm and dragging me towards the trees. 'They're Remote Operation Bio-location Observation and Termination units!'

'What?'

I glance back to see three glowing spheres hovering above our pop-up tent.

'Killer robots!' Dad shouts as a silent explosion of light engulfs the clearing. When the flash fades the tent is gone. 'Run!'

BZZZT!

'These robots are sent by the Cosmic Authority,' Dad whispers, keeping a tight grip on my arm as we hurry through the woods. 'Programmed to detect and eliminate any alien life forms found on this world.'

'Who is this Cosmic Authority?' I hiss, flinching as a leaf crunches noisily beneath my feet. I glance back to see if the strange lights are following us, but all I can see are the shadows of the trees.

'The Cosmic Authority enforces the laws of

the universe,' Dad explains. 'Following these rules, every alien civilization has managed to live in harmony for millions of years. But if the Cosmic Authority catches any aliens breaking the law, then *bzzzt!*'

I shiver as I remember the silent explosion of light that engulfed the tent and wonder what it would have felt like if we'd been inside.

'These are the things that vaporized my spaceship and they would have vaporized me too if I hadn't used the Quintessence to disguise myself as a human being. That's what these probes are looking for now – any biological signs of alien life.'

Peering ahead into the darkness, Dad silently motions for me to follow him as he starts to climb the track. Through the tree branches, I catch glimpses of the stars and try not to imagine the gaze of the Cosmic Authority, searching for us in the woods.

I still can't believe that everything my dad's been telling me is true. That aliens really exist.

And even crazier than this, that he's one too.

My heart jumps as a beam of blue-white light cuts through the trees, only metres away from where we were just standing. Static crackles through the air as we turn and run. Glancing back over my shoulder, I catch a glimpse of a glowing sphere zigzagging through the trees. Its phosphorescence fills the forest with strange shadows. It looks like one of these killer robots

is right on our trail.

'What's it doing?' I ask, struggling to keep ahead of the light as the path climbs even higher.

'It's trying to get a fix on our bio-data,' Dad explains, fiddling with the egg-shaped stone in his hand as he runs. 'Scanning for any trace of alien DNA.'

'But you said you used that device to reprogram your biology. If you've got human DNA now, why's it still following you?'

'It's not following me,' Dad replies as another blue-white beam crackles through the trees. 'It's following *you*.'

I glance back in fear, the glowing sphere shining brighter as the path starts to clear. It's getting closer and I feel every hair on my head standing on end. This doesn't make any sense. I'm from planet Earth, not Proxima b.

That's when everything Dad's been trying to tell me suddenly clicks into place in my head. Why gravity isn't anything to be scared of and the reason my skin turned bright green.

If my dad's an alien, what does that make me?

The path ahead is coming to an end and I see a large sign that says, 'FEEL THE SPHERE!'

'This way,' Dad says, pushing past a metal gate as the blue-white light flashes again.

As shock waves roll inside my brain, I stumble forward. I don't want to *feel the sphere*, but I've got no choice.

Following Dad through the gate, I suddenly see several large round shapes looming in the gloom. For one terrifying moment I think these are more killer robots, super-sized and hiding in the dark. But then I realize what they are.

'Zorbs!'

They look like giant hamster balls, squashed together behind the gate.

'Quick,' Dad says, grabbing hold of the nearest one and angling it towards me. 'Climb in.'

I stare into the hole on the side of the inflatable zorb as Dad holds it steady. There's no other way in and no time to argue as another blue-white beam cuts through the trees. Springing forward on my toes, I jump through the hole and slither inside the zorb. I scramble to my feet as Dad slides through the hole behind me, the transparent plastic squeaking as I try to stop myself from falling over.

'What are we doing?' I hiss, the sound of my voice almost too loud inside the enclosed space. 'I don't think this is a good time to go zorbing.'

Through the transparent plastic I can see the bright shapes of more glowing spheres hovering above the trees.

I glance back at my dad who's staring down at the pebble in the palm of his hand.

'Hiding,' he replies. 'The thick layer of compressed air inside this zorb should disguise our bio-data signals for a while. Long enough to get this thing working again, I hope.'

The faint lights of the Quintessence flicker with a pale pink glow.

'What's up with it?'

'When you activated the quantum flare, you drained the power cell,' Dad explains, gently stroking the pebble as if encouraging it back to life. 'If I can get the harmonic modulating circuit running, I'll be able to keep you safe – but I need more power.'

I look around to see if I can find something that will help. There are rubber straps, Velcro belts and handholds for passengers to grab on to, but I can't see any sign of a charging point for this piece of alien technology.

I'm about to ask my dad what he needs when a sudden flash of blue-white light almost blinds me. I screw my eyes shut against the glare, but when I open them again I see a trio of glowing spheres hovering outside the zorb.

They've found us.

i WANT TO GET OFF

Close up they look more like robots, silvery metallic shapes glinting inside the spheres of glowing light.

Fear coils inside my mind as I stare into the brightness. I want to move. I want to run. But we're trapped inside this inflatable idiot ball and there's nothing I can do.

There's a crackle of static and then I feel the air start to harden around us.

I turn towards my dad and see the look of panic spreading across his face too. Outside the inflatable globe, the three glowing spheres seem to brighten and I wince as I wait for the silent explosion of light. Dad said we'd find an A to Z of adventure here, but I didn't think this would mean being zapped by aliens while trapped in a zorb. Then I remember – it's my dad who's the alien, and maybe me too, but we're still stuck inside this zorb.

Suddenly an idea hits me out of nowhere; a lightning flash of inspiration that gets me reaching for the dangling straps. We don't need to get out of here to escape – we just need to *move*.

'Hold on tight,' I shout, poking my toes into the rubber footholds at the base of the zorb. I pull the Velcro belts across my shoulders and my stomach, pulling them tight as I try to strap myself in.

Realizing what I'm doing, Dad does the same. Facing each other, we grab hold of the handles on the opposite sides of the zorb's inner core, our arms and legs outstretched as we stand there defenceless. Through the transparent plastic, the blue-white light seems brighter than the moon and if we're going to do it, it has to be now.

'Let's go!'

Holding tight to the handles, we rock our bodies backwards and forwards as, with a reluctant squeaking noise, the zorb begins to move. It starts to roll forward, slowly at first, pushing open the metal gate as I feel myself turned upside down. The blood rushes to my head and then drains away almost immediately as the zorb continues to roll. I can hear the ground rumbling beneath us as the brightness fades away and is replaced by an onrushing dark.

We're picking up speed, the inflatable plastic squelching around us as the zorb careers down the slope. I seem to have left my stomach behind as the floor of the zorb turns into the ceiling and then back into the floor, over and over again. I feel like I'm spinning around a black hole, the gravity getting stronger as the giant ball bounces past the trees.

I want to get off.

My knuckles whiten as I cling to the handles, my mouth opening wide in a scream. But no sound comes out as I'm flipped over again and gravity pushes the scream back down my throat. I've made a mistake – being zapped by killer robots would've been a quicker way to die.

I catch a glimpse of my dad as we tumble over again and I see the massive grin on his face.

'WHEEEEEEEE!'

I don't believe it. He's actually enjoying this!

Every bump in the track sends the zorb flying higher. It feels like we're travelling at one hundred miles an hour, and through the plastic walls the darkness seems to blur. I don't know which way is up or down any more. The only thoughts left inside my head are a spin cycle of fear.

'Woo-hoo!' Dad shouts. 'Eat zorb dust, killer robots!'

The inflatable ball crashes into a bank, bouncing sideways as it clears the trees, and I catch a glimpse of the tents in the field.

Oh no. How are we going to stop?

Gravity takes control of my trousers as the zorb picks up speed again. Through the translucent plastic I see lights spiralling past and then a dark shape looms out of the gloom.

There's no way to avoid it as zorbs don't come fitted with brakes. Or a steering wheel. Basically, we're just going to bounce to our deaths. The words escape my lips in a high-pitched squeak.

'We're going to crash!'

SPLAT!

With a thumping jolt, the zorb squashes the tent flat. I feel the Velcro belts straining at my chest as our giant hamster ball of death caroms forward towards its final destination.

The campfire has been built in front of the yurt. As the world spins wildly round, I glimpse the dads and kids milling around the fire. I imagine before we crashed through the tent they were happily toasting their flying saucer marshmallows, but as the zorb bounces forward they now seem to be running and screaming in fear.

The zorb is speeding straight for the campfire and I realize I'm going to have to add being toasted to death to my list of ways in which this zorb is trying to kill me.

Straight ahead, I see Flip Foxley waving his arms wildly as he tries to get us to stop. His mouth seems to be moving, but I can't hear any words above the rumble of the zorb as we bounce forward across the grass.

'Get out of the way!' I shout.

For a second, Flip stands his ground, arms outstretched as though he thinks he can catch us. Then he seems to think better of this, diving to one side as the zorb hits a hummock and then soars straight over him.

A strange feeling of weightlessness comes over me as I watch the world tumbling by. Inside the zorb, Dad and I are spinning in a perfect orbit, the space between us disappearing as we fly through the air. Then I glimpse the roaring flames of the campfire and realize this is going to be rather a toasty landing.

But before we hit, a blinding light illuminates the zorb. I shut my eyes against the sudden glare and, when I dare to open them again, I see that we're hanging suspended in the air. Beneath my

DON'T PANIC!

'Don't panic!' Dad shouts as the compressed air splutters out with a sound like an elephant's fart. 'I've got this all under control.'

Wriggling free from the straps, I stare at him in horror as the blue-white beam cuts the air between us. The zorb is being sliced in two, each half slowly deflating as we're both held suspended in the light.

This must be some kind of tractor beam, but as I stare up into the blinding light I can't see where it's coming from.

'Jake!'

Glancing down, I see Damon and Amba running towards the campfire. Behind them, Flip is still picking himself up off the muddy ground, whilst everybody else stares up at the sky with their mouths open wide and camera phones held high.

'Keep back,' I shout. 'It's not safe.'

Actually, if I'm completely honest, being held prisoner in a tractor beam feels a teensy bit safer than zorbing through a forest at night with killer robots on your trail. But I still feel kind of worried about what's going to happen next.

I glance across at Dad who's fiddling with his device, seemingly unconcerned that he's currently hovering in mid-air on a deflating inflatable above a roaring campfire.

'What are you doing? What's happening?'

'I'm trying to get this to work,' he says, grappling with the egg-shaped stone as the lights on its surface flicker greyly. 'Then we'll be able to—'

A deafening sound cuts off the rest of his sentence.

DUN – DUN – DUUUN – DUUUNNNN – DUN!

I clap my hands to my ears, trying to block out the noise that seems to be falling from the sky.

'What's that?'

Dad mouths a reply but I can't hear his words as my ears are still ringing.

Beneath our feet, the deflated halves of the zorb slowly drift to the ground, smothering the flames of the campfire with a fizzling hiss. But we're still floating in mid-air, the blinding blue-white light flickering between us as if trying to make up its mind.

I stare up again, into the brightness, but I still can't see where this light is coming from. There are no stars in the sky, just an empty blackness broken only by this single beam. Then I realize the darkness isn't empty. There's something huge up there and it's filling the sky.

Then the rest of its lights come on.

'Wow!'

It looks just like the Easter Egg spaceship that Dad built at the school fete, but so, *so* much bigger. Its curving hull shimmers with countless points of lights, every single one of them dazzlingly bright. A galaxy of stars shines down out of the sky. But there is no sky any more, only this endless spaceship of glittering lights that looks as big as the world.

In the distance I can hear a dog barking, then the deafening tones sound out again.

DUN – DUN – DUUUN – DUUUNNNN – DUN!

The tractor beam is coming from the bottom of the spaceship, the blue-white rays now transformed into a rainbow of light.

'That's it!' Dad shouts as the colours fly around us. He holds up the Quintessence, the starry lights on its surface now shining with the same brightness as before. 'It's working again.'

But as he speaks I feel my fingers prickle with a strange sensation. Glancing down at my hands, I see a shimmering rainbow scrolling across my skin. I try to pull them out of the light, but find I can't move my hands. Horrified, I watch as the rainbow rays slowly start to crawl up my arms.

'Dad,' I shout, looking across to him for help. 'What's happening?'

He's standing in the same shimmering light, the shiny silver material of his ski suit now glittering with every colour under the sun.

'Inside the zorb, our bio-data signals were mingled,' Dad explains as he desperately twists the Quintessence between his fingers. 'They're scanning us again to find out who's the alien. And I'm going to show them that it's me.' He winces as the tiny device suddenly flares with a dazzling light. 'Catch.'

He tosses the egg-shaped pebble towards me. I watch as it cuts a silvery trail through the shimmer that surrounds us both now. Gritting my teeth, I thrust my hand forward to pluck the device out of the air before it falls past my fingers.

It feels strangely heavier than before. Close up, I can see that the dazzling light is made up of countless tiny stars. It looks like I'm holding the universe in the palm of my hand.

And then it starts.

I'm still trapped inside this shimmering rainbow, but something is happening to *me*. I feel like a jigsaw tipped out on to the floor, but where every piece of the puzzle is landing in exactly the right place. It's like every cell inside my body is singing a new melody, but the song somehow remains the same.

'Dad!'

'Don't worry, Jake!' Dad shouts, sagging slightly as the shimmering beam still holds him in its light. 'It'll realize that you're human now. I'm the one they're after.'

The beam of light dances between us, its colours constantly flickering blue, green, violet, orange, indigo, yellow and red. It's as though it can't decide what's right. And then the light that surrounds me suddenly turns a brilliant white and I feel myself dropped to the ground.

I land on the muddy grass, feeling my feet squelch as I look up to see my dad still held captive in the shimmering beam.

That's when I realize what he's done.

I'm still holding the Quintessence in my hand and I remember how Dad said this kept him safe when he first landed here on Earth. *'I went undercover as a human being. The harmonic modulating circuit reprogrammed my biology.'* That's why he had to get it working again. He's used it to change himself back.

DUN – DUN – DUUUN – DUUUNNNN – DUN!

The same deafening tones roll down from the sky, but this time these sounds turn to words inside my head.

CAUTION! SPACESHIP REVERSING!
CAUTION! SPACESHIP REVERSING!

I glance down at the Quintessence and remember what else Dad said that it did. *'This device is equipped with a universal translator.'* This must be why I can understand alien now.

'Jake!' Dad's voice sounds strained as he calls down to me. 'There's not much time left.'

I glance up again to see the shimmering beam has now turned to a sickly-green colour. And trapped inside this unearthly light, my dad seems to be turning into something else.

It's difficult to see exactly what's happening, the light almost blinding me. But Dad's skin now seems to be as green as this shimmering beam. I hold my breath, almost frightened to watch what happens next, but then I catch a glimpse of his face through the light and I realize . . .

He's still my dad.

I tighten my grip on the Quintessence. I've got to get this back to him. He's got to use it to disguise himself again.

'Dad,' I shout, pulling my arm back ready to throw it to him. 'You've got to change back.'

'It's too late,' Dad shouts, his words almost lost as the spaceship reversing message booms out of the sky again. 'The scan's finished now and they've got the result that they need. One alien life form captured. That'll be enough to keep the Cosmic Authority happy.'

The shimmering beam that surrounds Dad seems to brighten, his silhouette blurring with the light.

'There's so much I need to tell you, but there isn't any time. Use the Quintessence to keep you safe, but don't forget who you are. I never meant to embarrass you, Jake. All I ever wanted to do was help you reach for the stars.'

'Dad . . .'

I try to move towards the light, but feel hands dragging me back.

'Tell your mum I love her very much,' Dad calls out, his voice breaking as the shimmering beam turns into a supernova. 'And never forget that I love you too.'

Then I watch as the light shines right through him.

With a zipping sound, the shimmering beam disappears into the base of the spaceship.

I stare up in disbelief as the rest of its lights

blink out.

For a second, the darkness just hangs there. And then there's a noise that sounds like light being made and suddenly the stars come out again.

The spaceship is gone.

And so is my dad.

DAD'S NEVER COMING HOME

'Eyewitnesses claim that Ion Jones, a local man attending a Dads and Kids' Adventure Weekend *at the Getaway Experience with his ten-year-old son Jake, was "beamed up" into the UFO which then disappeared completely. However, all camera phone footage of this so-called "alien encounter" in Middlewich Forest seems to have been mysteriously wiped. Authorities suspect that the incident may be some kind of hoax, as a viral video now being shared on social media shows the same man chasing a runaway Lego spaceship at a local school fete. But this evening, there is no escaping the fact that Ion Jones is still missing and, as I stand outside the Jones's family home, a young boy inside is missing his dad.'*

Stabbing my thumb down on the remote I angrily switch off the TV, but I can still hear the sound of the reporter's voice.

Getting up off the sofa, I make my way over to the window. The living-room curtains are already drawn, even though it's only just gone dark outside, but peeking through a gap I can just see the back of the TV newsman as he wraps up his report.

And he's not the only one out there.

It looks like most of the world's media is camped outside our front gate. I can see their names on the sides of the vans which fill the street: BBC, ITV, CNN, 5 Live, Sky News and even North West Tonight. Beneath the street lights a small forest of TV cameras crowds the pavement, their lenses all aimed straight at my house. As the first reporter puts down his microphone, I watch as a second news crew starts to set up their shot, the reporter bustling her way to an empty spot next to the wheelie bins.

It's been like this ever since I got back from the woods.

The police brought me home, but even as they told Mum what I said had happened to Dad, I could tell they didn't believe a word.

Strange lights in the sky. Unidentified Flying Object. No sign of your husband anywhere.

The others at the campsite tried to prove that what I was saying was true. But all of their camera phone videos came out blank and the one photo that Amba's dad took of the spaceship just showed a few blurry lights in the sky. And when the policewoman asked what Dad was wearing when he went missing and I described his shiny ski suit, she couldn't stop herself from smiling.

'So your dad was dressed as a spaceman when he was beamed up by these aliens?' she said.

Reluctantly, I nodded my head. But I didn't tell her that my dad was an alien too.

Still peering through the curtains, my gaze drifts up from the TV news crews to the darkening sky above the roofs of the houses on our street. The stars are beginning to come out and, as I blink back my tears, I wonder where my dad is now.

A sudden flash makes me jump in surprise. Then I see the photographer leaning over the garden fence, his camera lens pointing straight towards me. The camera flashes again and I quickly close the crack in the curtains.

Everyone's desperate to get the first pictures and interview with the kid who says his dad was abducted by aliens. Mum's stopped answering the door. She says they'll all get bored and go away soon, but I can't help worrying that if they do that'll mean that Dad's never coming home.

Slumping down on the sofa, the leather squeaks as I reach forward to pick up my rucksack. Inside this is everything I brought back from the woods. Unzipping the bag, I start to pull out my stuff, throwing my muddy clothes on to the floor as I search for the thing I've hidden in here. Then I stop as my hand closes round a bundled-up pair of Dad's smelly socks.

I'd already packed my rucksack ready to leave when the killer robots turned up. I'd left this on the grass when we ran into the woods, but when the robots disintegrated the pop-up tent they destroyed all of Dad's stuff. Except for these socks. They must've got mixed up with my clothes when I was packing up.

I hold the socks in my hand. They still smell rather cheesy, but that's not what's making my eyes water now. Unbundling them, I pull out the Quintessence from the place where I'd hidden it away, safely wrapped up inside Dad's smelly socks.

Resting it in the palm of my hand, I stare at the strange egg-shaped device. There's no sign of the dazzling light that shone out of it back in the woods. Now it lies lifeless in the centre of my palm, its stone-like surface as black as my mood.

Everyone wants proof that aliens exist. Well, I've got this.

Dad told me this was real alien technology. He said this device saved his life when he first landed here on Earth and he used it to save mine. I blink back my tears as I remember being trapped in the tractor beam – Dad frantically twisting the Quintessence between his fingers before throwing it to me. I remember how the stars shone as I felt it changing something inside me and the sinking feeling I got as I glanced up to see Dad changing too.

It looked like he was turning into something else, his skin glowing green in the light. But the light was too bright for me to see exactly what this was. Lizard man? Space frog? Alien blob? The questions whirl around my brain. Is that what's going to happen to me when I hit puberty?

Only Dad knows, but he could be half the universe away by now. I've got to get him back and I've got an idea how.

Inside this Quintessence is an emergency distress signal – a quantum flare. When I accidentally set this off in the woods it brought the spaceship back, so that's what I've got to do now. I twist the device between my fingers, waiting for the click that will tell me that it's worked.

Nothing happens.

I try twisting the device in the opposite direction, but there's still no click. No lights flicker across its surface. No quantum flare activates to tell the universe that I'm here. My fingers twist and probe the egg-shaped device, but whatever I do I can't seem to find the right switch. Has it run out of charge again?

Frustrated, I try and shake the pebble into life, but the smooth black stone stays silent in my hand.

It's not working.

The aliens aren't coming back and neither is my dad.

I hear the living-room door start to open and quickly wipe my eyes with the back of my sleeve. And when I look up, Mum's standing there with a mug in her hand.

'I've brought you a cup of tea.'

TWO HEARTS

'Why didn't you tell me the truth?'

Mum always says a cup of tea is the answer to everything, but as steam rises from the mug she doesn't seem to have an answer to this question.

She shakes her head as she places the mug of tea on the coffee table in front of me.

'We wanted to tell you the truth, Jake,' Mum says, looking tired as she sits down on the sofa by my side. 'But we were waiting for the right time. It's not the easiest thing in the world to reveal that the man you married is actually from another planet.'

I'm not sure why, but hearing Mum say these words out loud fills me with surprise. I suppose it's because she's always been the sensible one. Whenever Dad was getting up to one of his crazy tricks, Mum was always the one I could count on. The parent I could trust. But now I know she's been keeping the biggest secret in the world from me.

'How long have you known?'

'Pretty much from the moment I first met him,' Mum replies, the corners of her mouth creasing in a sad smile.

Mum and Dad always told me that they met at work. Well, Mum was at work in her ambulance. Dad was in a road accident. It was Mum's ambulance that rushed him to hospital.

'When your dad was run over, I was the first paramedic on the scene—' Mum explains as she starts telling me the story I've heard a hundred times before.

'I know, I know,' I interrupt, eager to avoid all the gooey romantic stuff. 'Dad always says that you saved his life and stole his heart.'

'That's right,' Mum replies, looking slightly annoyed at being interrupted. 'But Dad never told you that I was the one who ran him over.'

I stare at Mum, astonished. 'What do you mean?'

'It was twelve years ago. I'd just started working as a paramedic when my ambulance was called out to a report of an accident near Middlewich Forest. Someone said they'd seen a light aircraft crashing in the woods. We were nearly there, sirens blaring, when your dad just walked out of the woods into the middle of the road. The ambulance knocked him flying and, to be honest, I thought we'd killed him. But when I raced to Ion's side to check his vital signs, I noticed that he seemed to look rather green.'

She nods towards the Quintessence that's resting on the table in front of us.

'Your dad was holding that thing tightly in his hand, and when I touched his chest it suddenly shone with a glittering light. I didn't know what to do as I watched it turn his skin from green to pink, so quickly I thought I must've been imagining it. And then your dad opened his eyes.'

Mum's own eyes are shining now, but she doesn't let these tears get in the way of her explanation.

'Ion told me that he was lost and alone and so, so far from home. Beneath my fingers, I could feel a double-thud inside his chest. Two hearts beating at the same time. And then they stopped.'

Mum reaches up to wipe her tears away.

'My training kicked in, I gave Ion emergency CPR and somehow got him breathing again. We had to race to get him to hospital, but in the back of the ambulance he told me the truth. How he was an alien who had just landed here and how he needed my help to survive. Ion told me that he was being hunted by a creature called the Cosmic Authority who wouldn't rest until it had captured him. And now I know he was right.'

Mum reaches out for my hand.

'Your dad and I fell in love, and when you came along this gave us even more of a reason to keep our secret. We just wanted to keep you safe, Jake.'

I blink back my own tears as I remember Dad disappearing into the shimmering beam of light.

'You should've *told* me.'

'That's why Dad took you to Middlewich Forest. He just wanted the chance to spend some time with you in order to tell you the truth at last. He thought it would make sense if he showed you the place where it all began.'

'I thought you said he wanted to say sorry for embarrassing me.'

I feel Mum's fingers gently tighten round mine as she squeezes my hand.

'Your dad never means to embarrass you, Jake. He just gets things wrong sometimes. It's because he doesn't always understand how things work here on Earth. That's why he used to give you a raw onion instead of an apple in your lunch box for school. It was my fault for telling him to make sure you got your five fruit and veg a day. He didn't know you weren't supposed to eat raw onions.'

I remember how all the other kids laughed

when I opened my lunch box. Right now I'd eat a hundred raw onions to bring my dad back home.

'Where do you think they've taken him?' I ask, my voice sounding so small as I remember the huge spaceship that beamed him up.

Mum shakes her head. 'I don't know. Maybe back to his home planet. But your dad won't like that. When we first got together, I used to ask him what life was like there. Honestly, Jake, it sounded so dull. There's no music or art, songs or stories – not like here on Earth. Your dad told me that most aliens think facts are all that matter. That's why he never fitted in. He said it was only when he heard the songs that Earth was singing that he realized he wasn't alone. Every feeling he'd kept hidden inside was entwined within a melody. Songs that make you happy, songs that let you be sad – a soundtrack for every possible emotion and music that makes you dance. Everyone's connected when they hear the song. That's why your dad loves to sing, Jake – it makes him feel like he belongs.'

The loud ring of the front doorbell makes us both jump.

'That's it,' Mum says, her eyes still shining as she climbs to her feet. 'If that's one of those reporters again, I'm going to give them a piece of my mind.'

As Mum hurries to answer the front door, I hear the sound of a knock coming from the back. More reporters, I bet. And this time *I* can tell them to get lost.

Racing to the kitchen, I open the back door to see Damon and Amba standing there. Amba smiles at me, whilst Damon looks around nervously from underneath his hood. It's not even raining.

'Hi, Jake.'

The last time I saw them both was back in the forest when Dad got beamed up into the spaceship. Right after they laughed at me for looking like a swamp monster from Mars. That was when everything started to go wrong. I'm not even sure if I want to be their friend any more.

'What do you want?'

'We want to say we're sorry, Jake,' Amba replies, tugging on the straps of the rucksack she's wearing as if it's too heavy for her back. 'And we want to help rescue your dad. Can we come in?'

THE ALIENS HAVE GOT
THESE PROBES

Amba empties her rucksack on to the kitchen table and my heart slowly sinks as the books spill out. Pictures of flying saucers and little green men stare out from the plastic-backed covers and a quick glance at the titles confirms my very worst fears:

UFO: FACT OR FICTION?

EXTRATERRESTRIAL ENCOUNTERS

MYSTERIES FROM THE SKY

SECRETS OF THE MEN IN BLACK

THE TRUTH ABOUT AREA 51
THE ALIENS ARE COMING!

'What are all these books?' I ask.

The three of us are sitting round the kitchen table, glasses of juice and a plate of home-made biscuits left out for us by my mum.

'Research,' Amba replies as Damon tucks into a biscuit. 'We went to the library and asked for every book they had on aliens and UFOs.'

'This isn't some school project, Amba,'

I say, pushing the books back towards her. 'This is serious.'

'Don't let Mrs Beale hear you say that,' Damon says through a mouthful of biscuit. 'She made me do my last project on "Animals of the Sea" all over again because she said it showed poor research skills. I didn't know whales didn't lay eggs. Can you imagine the size of them if they did?'

Raising an eyebrow at Damon's fishy confession, Amba picks up the nearest of the books. On its front cover, I see a picture of a silvery alien with saucer-shaped eyes beneath the title: THE ALIEN HUNTER'S HANDBOOK: All You Need to Know about Outer Space Invaders.

'I am taking it seriously,' Amba says as she flicks through its pages. 'But if we want to get your dad back, we've got to find out why the aliens have taken him. According to this book, thousands of people every year are kidnapped by aliens but the government keeps this all hushed up.'

She turns the book round so I can see the heading at the top of the page she's found.

ALIEN ABDUCTION: THE FACTS

'Let's assume they haven't exterminated him,' Amba continues, her pointing finger passing over an image of a bug-eyed alien armed with a laser blaster. 'Now, some alien species apparently treat coming to Earth like a trip to the supermarket to pick up some tasty treats, whilst others abduct humans to work as slaves on their remote alien ant farms.'

Across the table, Damon's face is turning the same shade as the little green man on the front of the book. It looks like he's going to be sick.

Reaching up, Amba twists a stray strand of curly black hair around her fingertip. 'Most humans, though, are taken for experimentation,' she continues. 'It's happened loads of times before. There are reports from all across the world. Most of the time the person is only taken for a day or two, but sometimes they can be gone for years. It says here that the aliens have got these probes that they—'

'Amba, stop,' Damon manages to croak.

'I'm only reading out what the book says,' Amba replies crossly. She turns and looks at me sympathetically. 'I'm not saying your dad *is* being experimented on, Jake.'

I think about what Dad has told me. How the universe is teeming with alien life. How these aliens think the human race is primitive and want to keep us away from the rest of the galaxy. How my dad is an alien who came to Earth twelve years ago.

I take a deep breath.

'There's something I need to tell you,' I say.

70,000 YEARS SOUNDS
LIKE FOR EVER

Amba stares at me with her eyes open wide. 'So your dad's an alien?' she says.

I nod my head.

'And this giant spaceship that beamed him up belongs to some kind of intergalactic police officer?'

I nod my head again.

'The Cosmic Authority,' I reply.

'Is your mum an alien too?' Damon asks, now looking suspiciously at the plate of home-baked biscuits on the table.

I shake my head. 'No,' I say, feeling kind of relieved that Mum's gone upstairs for a lie-down now. 'My mum's human – she met my dad here on Earth.'

Damon turns his head towards me, searching my face as if he expects me to turn green again.

'So what does that make you?'

I think about this, trying to work it out for myself. My dad's an alien. My mum's a human being. What *does* that make me?

'I . . . I don't know,' I stutter.

Even though I'm sitting still, I feel my heart begin to race. I can almost hear a double-thud of heartbeats, thundering away inside my chest. I feel like I'm falling into a black hole.

Amba reaches out to take my hand. 'It makes you Jake,' she says, kicking Damon under the table. 'And you're our friend.'

'Ow, Amba!' Damon protests. Then he catches sight of the fierce glare that Amba's aiming in his direction. 'Oh yeah. Sorry, Jake.

I didn't mean anything bad by that. I think it's cool you've got an alien for a dad.'

'My dad isn't cool,' I sigh. 'In fact, most of the time he's really embarrassing. But I still want him back.'

'Don't worry,' Amba says, giving my hand a friendly squeeze before letting it go. 'We're going to get your dad back.'

'But how are we going to do that?' Damon asks. 'That spaceship might be halfway to Mars by now.'

'My dad doesn't come from Mars. He's from a planet called . . .' I pause as I remember the strange noise that Dad made when he said its name and decide to go with the Earth version instead, 'Proxima b.'

Amba makes a sudden excited noise. 'I read about Proxima b in the library!'

Picking up another of the books, Amba quickly flicks through it until she finds the page she's looking for and then begins to read out loud.

'Nowadays, astronomers can use telescopes to search for alien worlds where life might exist. By analysing the light emitted by a star, it's possible to detect whether any planets are in orbit around it and even whether these "exoplanets" might be capable of supporting life. The closest exoplanet astronomers have found so far is called Proxima b and is located only four point two light years away from Earth. However, using current technology, it would take a spacecraft seventy thousand years to reach Proxima b, so there's little chance of us popping round to say hello to any new alien neighbours who might be living there.'

Amba looks up and I see the disappointment on her face.

'I'm sorry, Jake.'

4.2 light years doesn't sound very far away. But 70,000 years sounds like for ever.

I feel like I'm going to cry.

Reaching into my pocket for a tissue to stop my eyes from leaking, my fingers find something egg-shaped there instead. I pull this out, placing it on the table in front of Amba.

'What's this?' she asks.

The jet-black pebble sits there lifeless.

'Alien technology,' I reply. 'My dad called it the Quintessence.'

'What does it do?' Damon asks.

'Loads of stuff,' I reply. 'My dad used it to disguise himself as a human when he first landed here on Earth. It can translate alien languages and even has a quantum flare that can send a distress signal across the universe. I thought I could use this to lure the spaceship back.'

With a thoughtful look on her face, Amba picks up the device.

'It's supposed to light up when you twist it between your fingers,' I tell her. 'But it doesn't seem to work any more.'

Holding it up to her eye, Amba peers at the egg-shaped pebble. 'Clockwise or anti-clockwise?' she asks.

'I don't know. Either way, I think, but neither seem to work now. I think my dad must have left the safety catch on.'

I watch as Amba tries to twist the Quintessence, her hands moving in opposite directions. For a second, I hold my breath, fingers crossed, hoping that the starry lights on the stone will shimmer into life again.

But nothing happens. Not even a faint glimmer of light can be seen. The alien device still looks like a dull, black pebble.

Amba hands it back to me.

'I thought if I could send a signal then the aliens would come back.' I look down at the useless device. 'I guess I was wrong.'

Silence descends as the three of us sit glumly around the kitchen table. No more bright ideas. No chance of getting my dad back.

'That's it!' Amba snaps her fingers, the sudden sound of this making Damon jump in surprise. 'Maybe there's another kind of signal we could send that would bring the aliens back.'

'What do you mean?' I ask.

Beneath her curly fringe, Amba's brown eyes shine with excitement. 'Didn't you say aliens aren't allowed to come to Earth?'

I nod my head. 'Dad said it was strictly forbidden.'

'So if we could send a signal that shows there is *another* alien here on Earth, the Cosmic Authority would have to come and get him, right?'

'I suppose so, but how are we supposed to do that?'

Then the front doorbell rings again.

'Go away!' I hear my mum shout from upstairs. 'And take your TV cameras with you too!'

Momentarily distracted, I turn back towards Amba and then notice the strange way she seems to be looking at me.

'What?'

Amba grins in a way that suddenly makes me feel kind of worried.

'I've got an idea,' she says.

MY DAD ALWAYS TOLD ME NOT TO EAT MY GREENS

I stare at the glass that's standing on the kitchen table in front of me, filled to the brim with an evil-looking mulch of murky green slime. The rest of the table is strewn with vegetable scraps: broccoli stalks and

asparagus ends, sprout peelings and shredded spinach leaves, but the rest of this vegetable tsunami has all been blended to a pulp and poured into this brimming glass of goo.

'There you are, Jake,' Amba announces, taking away the now-empty blender jug, its insides splattered with the same green slime. 'One Super Vegetable Smoothie Shake with added Vitamin C – all ready to drink.'

My stomach turns as I look more closely at the drink, now seeing the bits floating in it.

Earlier this year, our teacher, Mrs Beale, took us pond dipping in the local park. Using our nets, we skimmed the pond and then deposited what we'd collected in our trays, although Frankie Baines spent most of his time flicking us all with slime. I remember the sludgy mess that filled up my observation tray, pond weed and slimy creatures wriggling through the goo. We had to use this worksheet to work out what we'd caught, and I discovered that my tray was mostly filled with fly larvae and water flea soup.

But this crazy super shake that Damon and Amba have made me looks even more disgusting.

'Come on, Jake,' Damon says, giving me an encouraging smile. 'Drink up.'

I shake my head. 'This isn't going to work.'

'I think it will,' Amba replies, setting the jug on the side and turning round to face me again. 'When your skin turned green on the Kidsplorers weekend, you said it was an allergic reaction to the broccoli soup that you drank. The same thing happens to your dad too and, if you're both chlorophyll-intolerant, then maybe this comes from the alien part of you.'

Stepping closer, Amba looks at me with a serious expression on her face.

'Every vegetable we've put in this drink is chock-full of chlorophyll so it's bound to trigger the same reaction. If we want the Cosmic Authority to think you're breaking his stupid rules then you need to look the part. We need you to turn green, Jake. We need you to look like an alien.'

I look up at my friend. What she's saying sounds so convincing, but the truth is I'm scared.

Most parents are always nagging their kids to eat their vegetables, but since I was little my dad always told me *not* to eat my greens. And now I know why.

I remember watching him caught in the tractor beam, his skin glowing green in the light. If I ever want to see him again, I've got to do this.

Closing my eyes so I can't see the slime, I lift the glass to my lips and start to drink.

As the sloppy green goo pours down my throat, I gag.

It might've looked disgusting but it tastes even worse. I feel my stomach turn, a spin cycle of nausea whirring into life. I can taste sprouts and broccoli, peas, spinach and celery, the odd stray leaf that's mixed in with the slime almost making me choke.

And then the last drop drains from the glass and I bang it down on the table in front of me.

Breathing hard to stop myself from being sick, I look up at my friends.

'How do I look?' I ask, trying to ignore the washing machine that's churning in my stomach. 'Has it worked?'

Looking stunned, Damon and Amba don't say a word. Instead Amba holds up her pocket mirror and I stare into it to see a strange alien face staring back at me. My skin glows with a weird greenish tinge and, as my mouth gapes wide in surprise, I can see that even my tongue has turned green.

'It's worked,' Amba says, finally re-membering how to speak. 'Now we just need to show the world.'

SMELLY SOCKS!

Crouching down in front of the front door, Damon flips open the letter box.

'They're still all there,' he says as he peers out at the TV news crews gathered outside my front gate.

As I listen to the hubbub of voices outside, I feel a panicky fluttering inside my chest. It almost feels like two hearts are beating in there. Lifting my hand, I press my green fingers against my chest to try to calm my runaway nerves.

'I still don't see how embarrassing me in

front of the whole world is going to bring the Cosmic Authority back.'

'When you go out there,' Amba says, taking my hand in hers as my heartbeat starts to slow, 'those TV cameras aren't just going to be beaming pictures of you around the world. Those signals will head out into space too, travelling at the speed of light. In one of those library books it said we've been sending signals into space ever since we invented TV and radio. All the TV programmes we watch and all the songs we hear on the radio escape from Earth's atmosphere and travel to the stars.'

I remember what Dad told me about the sphere of silence that is placed around our solar system, blocking out all the TV and radio signals that we send. But one signal got through before – the message that brought Dad to Earth. The loneliest voice he'd ever heard, singing 'Space Oddity'.

'That's how you can tell the Cosmic Authority that Ion's your dad,' Amba continues, letting go of my hand as she reaches for the door handle. 'And if he thinks you're an alien too, he's going to come back and beam you up.'

It sounds like Amba has thought of everything. I just need to hope that huge spaceship hasn't left the solar system by now. I shiver as I remember the rainbow beam of its scanner, scrolling across my skin. Then I remember something else.

'There's just one problem,' I say. Reaching into my pocket, I pull out the Quintessence and hold this up for Amba to see. 'I think my dad used this to reprogram my biology. When that spaceship scanned me at the campsite it thought I was a human being. My skin might be green, but an allergic reaction to a Super Vegetable Smoothie Shake isn't going to fool any extraterrestrial scanning machine.'

Amba's brow furrows in a frown. She looks at me thoughtfully. 'Tell me again why you and your dad hid in the zorb.'

'He said it would keep us disguised,' I say.

'Inside the zorb our bio-data signals were all mixed up so the Cosmic Authority couldn't tell which one of us was the alien.'

'Hmmm,' Amba says. 'So we need to mix up you and your dad's bio-data again. Maybe we could get some of his DNA – you know, like in the films when they use this to track the criminal down.'

'My dad's not a criminal!'

'No, but he *is* an alien,' Amba replies patiently. 'Have you got one of his hats or maybe a pair of gloves? Anything that might have a trace of his DNA. Preferably something a bit . . . smelly?'

I think about this for a moment. Mum's upstairs, so I can't go rooting around in their wardrobe. And all the clothes in Dad's rucksack were disintegrated when the killer robots blew up our tent. Except for his . . .

'Smelly socks!'

I race to get these from the living room.

'So what should I do with these?' I ask,

holding the socks well away from my nose. 'Do you want me to wear them?'

Amba nods her head as she plucks the socks out of my hand. 'Yes,' she says. 'But not on your feet.'

Reaching up to my head, Amba hooks a smelly sock over each ear.

'There,' she says as I feel the elasticated tops of the socks ping around my ears. 'Now when the aliens scan you, the first thing they'll read is your dad's DNA. You'll look and *smell* like an alien.'

I blink as my eyes start to water.

An invisible cloud of blue cheese and toenails now seems to be hanging in the air around my head. These socks really stink.

Holding his nose, Damon steps back from the front door to let me through. 'Good luck, Jake,' he says, his voice coming out in a nasally squeak.

'Just remember,' Amba says as I pause at the door. 'This will be the biggest news story ever. Real proof that aliens exist. Every TV channel will cut to show the news live, beaming your face up into space. There's no way the Cosmic Authority will be able to ignore this signal.'

My hand trembles as I reach for the front door handle. Through the obscured glass at the top of the door, I can see the bright lights of the TV cameras.

I'm not just going to embarrass myself in front of the whole world – I'm going to embarrass myself in front of the whole universe.

Taking a deep breath, I open the front door and step outside.

ARE WE STILL LIVE?

The cameras start flashing the moment I step out of the front door.

'That must be him!'

I feel my heart thumping in my chest, beating double time as I walk down the path. I can hear the reporters shouting out questions to me as the camera crews scramble to get into position.

'Where's your dad, Jake?'

'What happened at Middlewich Forest?'

'Did you really see a UFO?'

It's only short walk from my front door

to the gate, but every step I take seems to take longer and longer. Glancing back over my shoulder I see Damon and Amba peering through the letter box, but they can't help me now. I'm on my own.

Opening the front gate, I squeeze past the wheelie bins. To be honest, they don't smell any worse than Dad's socks. As I step out on to the street, the nearest of the reporters thrusts her microphone under my nose.

'Asha Barnes,' she says. 'BBC News. Jake, what can you tell us about what happened to your dad?'

I squint as I gaze up into the glare of the TV cameras. Every lens is pointing straight at me. My face might be bright green, but it's burning with embarrassment. I can see the reporter is looking at me suspiciously, her gaze taking in the green sheen of my skin.

'Jake,' she says again, more softly this time. 'Is there something you want to tell us?'

My throat feels dry, the words I've got to

say dying on my lips. Instead I nod my head and feel the socks on my ears flop back and forth.

I look into the lens of the nearest camera, the little green light on its side telling me it's transmitting live. The pictures it's sending are travelling all around the world. And maybe out into space too.

I take a deep breath.

'I'm here to tell the world the truth,' I say, trying to stop my voice from shaking. 'The truth is that our planet isn't the only planet where intelligent life exists.'

I look up into the darkened sky, the stars almost invisible beyond the glare of the TV lights. I try to remember what Dad told me when we were sitting together outside the pop-up tent.

'We're spinning round the Sun, but every star up there is a sun too,' I say, pointing up towards the darkness of the sky. 'All those stars have planets spinning round them, just like this one. Millions, billions, trillions of worlds. Why should we be so big-headed to think that Earth is the only world where life got clever?'

I turn to look at the reporter, her furry microphone still hovering under my nose.

'The universe is a very big place,' I say. 'And it's full of aliens.'

There's a moment of silence, filled only by the clicking of cameras. Then Asha Barnes coughs to clear her throat.

'And how exactly do you know this?' she asks. 'Did the aliens who took your dad tell you this?'

I shake my head.

'No. The aliens want to keep it a secret. They think we're too primitive to mix with the rest of the universe. They're keeping our planet locked away from the rest of the galaxy. It's against the law to even visit Earth. That's why they kidnapped my dad—'

'Wait a minute,' she interrupts. 'Are you trying to tell me your dad's been abducted by aliens? Looking for humans to experiment on with their probes, I suppose?'

With a glance at the camera, Asha Barnes shakes her head with a mocking smile. I can tell that she doesn't believe a word that I'm saying, but I've got to make the truth heard. It's my only chance to get my dad back. If this broadcast can make it to the stars, then I've got a message that the Cosmic Authority needs to hear.

'My dad's not human,' I say, staring straight down the camera lens. 'He's an alien who came to Earth twelve years ago. He met my mum, they fell in love and then they had me. Jake Jones. Human mum, alien dad, so if the Cosmic Authority is watching this—'

The reporter makes a throat-cutting gesture, pulling the microphone away before I can finish my sentence. 'I think we're finished here, guys,' she says to her camera crew. 'It's pretty obvious the kid's making it all up. I mean, just look at all this fancy dress make-up that he's wearing.

I bet his dad's put him up to this for some kind of publicity stunt.'

Shaking her head in disappointment, Asha Barnes starts to turn away.

'No, wait!' I call out. 'I can prove that what I'm saying is true.'

With fumbling fingers I reach into my pocket and pull out the Quintessence. I hold the egg-shaped device up to the light, hoping that all the TV cameras can get a close look at this alien technology.

'This is the Quintessence,' I say. 'It's what my dad used to survive here on Earth. It's the ultimate in alien technology. It can translate any language, make you invisible and even change your biology.'

I twist my fingers around the stone, listening for the click that will bring the Quintessence to life. But instead I hear the worst sound in the world.

Laughter.

Everyone's laughing.

I look up to see Asha Barnes hiding her face behind her hand, unable to disguise her giggles. Behind her I see the other reporters and camera operators, their shoulders shaking with laughter too. And it's not just the TV people – I can see my neighbours standing out in the street, pointing with flabbergasted grins.

Everyone's laughing at me.

As I stand there, my skin glowing green beneath the lights of the TV cameras, I feel my eyes start to leak.

It's all gone wrong.

The socks on my ears droop as I stare up into the darkness of the sky.

Just above the horizon I see a glowing orange beacon of light, brighter than any star. Inside my heart, a tiny spark of hope flickers into life. But then I realize what I'm looking at. This isn't a spaceship. It's Mars.

The tiny spark of hope flickers and fades.

I hear the TV news crews start to pack their gear away, the bright lights that lit the pavement in front of my house slowly going out one by one. I stay standing there in the growing darkness, my gaze still turned to the sky.

I can see the stars now and, through my tears, wonder which one is my dad's.

Maybe it's that bright blue-white star I can see in the middle of the sky. Dad said it was only four light years away. And then I realize – this star is getting bigger.

I hold my breath as I watch the bright star turn into a glowing sphere, its blue-white light shining down on me as I stare up in wonder.

'Look!'

This cry of surprise comes from Asha Barnes, but my eyes stay fixed on the glowing sphere. I realize now that this isn't one sphere but three, their glowing shapes slowly separating as they descend out of the darkness. As they get closer I start to see the silvery metallic shapes hidden in the light and, with a gulp, remember what Dad told me. *'They're Remote Operation Bio-location Observation and Termination units!'*

Killer robots.

I want to run, but my feet stay fixed to the pavement as the glowing spheres grow bigger and bigger.

'Are we still live?' I hear the TV reporter shout, her stunned voice incredulous. 'Are you getting these things on camera?'

A sudden crackle of static makes the hairs on the back of my neck stand on end. I'm still holding the pebble-shaped Quintessence, the starry lights on its surface now flickering into life.

The trio of glowing spheres are hovering over my head, filling my eyes with a dazzling brightness.

And then I hear a shout.

'Jake!'

Glancing back over my shoulder, I catch sight of my mum racing down the garden path.

'It's OK, Mum,' I shout. 'I've got this all under con—'

A beam of blue-white light suddenly splits the sky, engulfing me in a shimmering brightness. I can't speak. I can't even move a muscle as the light surrounds me, inside and out.

Frozen, I watch as flickering colours dance across my body, the shimmering light changing from blue to green to yellow to red, flashes of orange, violet and indigo travelling from the tips of my toes to the socks on my ears. I know what's happening. I'm being scanned; my bio-data read by the Cosmic Authority. I only hope Amba's plan works.

From what seems like a million miles away,

I hear the faint sound of the TV reporter's voice, her voice fuzzy in my ears as the static crackles again.

'Look at that! Look! At! That!'

I stare up into the brightness, but all I can see is the light. And then the light turns green.

I remember what happened to my dad and watch with a strange fascination as the same thing happens to me. The ghostly green glow of the beam seems to be brightening, the light shining right through me now. I don't feel any pain, but somewhere in the distance I hear the sound of Mum's voice calling out my name.

'Jake—'

Then I feel myself zipped out of existence.

THERE'S NO WAY WE CAN ESCAPE

'**O**w! Ow! Ow! Ow! Ow!'

I jump around as my feet hit the ground, the sensation of being zipped in and out of existence not much different to that time when I got my wotsits caught in the zip of my home-made pyjamas.

I mean, who puts a zip on a pair of pyjama bottoms?

My dad, that's who, and it's his voice I hear now as the pain of being beamed up slowly fades to a dull nagging ache.

'Jake?'

I look up to see my dad standing right in front of me. He's still dressed in his silly silver ski suit, the pong from this almost as bad as his socks as he stares at me in shock and surprise. He looks just the same as he usually does, but with one tiny difference. Just like me, his skin is bright green.

'What happened to you?' he exclaims. 'And why have you got my socks on your head?'

Reaching up, I quickly slide the socks off my ears and stuff these into my pocket.

'It was Amba's idea,' I explain. 'She said I needed to look like a proper alien to fool the Cosmic Authority. She made me a Super Smoothie Shake using every vegetable in the fridge and, when I drank it, an allergic reaction turned my skin bright green. We popped your smelly socks over my ears to disguise my bio-data, then I popped outside to tell the whole world who I really was on live TV and challenged the Cosmic Authority to come and get me. I didn't think it had worked at first, but then the spaceship came and beamed me up. And now I can rescue you.'

I grin, waiting for Dad to tell me how brilliant I am.

'You idiot!' he says, slapping his hands to his head in frustration. 'You should have listened to me, Jake. I told you to use the Quintessence

to keep you *safe*, but now you're trapped on this spaceship with me.'

'We don't have to be trapped,' I say, feeling rather annoyed at my dad's reaction to being rescued. 'We can escape together.'

With a despairing sigh, Dad throws his arms wide. 'And how exactly do you think we're going to do that?'

I look around the space, taking in my surroundings for the very first time.

It's not much bigger than the inside of the zorb. But instead of a translucent hue, the colour of this room is a bright electric blue. Every surface is smooth – the walls, ceiling and floor all curving at the sides and the edges. I can't see any windows or doors.

I try to push my hand against the nearest wall but feel my hand glide right past the surface without even making contact.

'What is this?' I ask, trying to push again against the gleaming blue sunshine. 'Where are we?'

'We're in a holding cell,' Dad explains. 'This is a bioengineered prison. The quantum teleportation beam that brought you on board scanned your bio-data, just like it did mine. Any other creature could walk right through this electromagnetic barrier, but there's no way we can escape.'

To demonstrate, Dad reaches out with his own hand and I watch as his green fingers bounce off the electric blue surface. He turns towards me, the lines around his tired eyes creased in concern.

'I wish you'd listened to me, Jake. You've put yourself in terrible danger being here.'

Dad rests his hands on my shoulders, and inside my brain I feel my rescue plan slowly falling to pieces. I spent so long worrying about how to find my dad again that I forgot to think about the most important bit – how I was actually going to rescue him.

If only I had a sonic screwdriver, like Doctor Who, that we could use to blast our way out of this place. Then I remember, I've got something even better than that.

Reaching into my pocket I pull out the Quintessence, noticing as I do that the green tinge on my fingers is already starting to fade.

'If it's our bio-data that's keeping us prisoner here, then why don't we use the Quintessence to reprogram our biology? It can make you human again and change me back too.'

Faint lights flicker across the surface of the egg-shaped stone but as I hold it out for my dad to take, he shakes his head sadly.

'It's no use, Jake,' he says, his gaze flicking over the device as he turns it over in his hands. 'These lights show that the Quintessence is currently running on auxiliary power. This means only its most basic functions are operational. The quantum flare isn't working, there's no cloaking shield and the harmonic modulating circuit is on the blink.' He hands the device back to me. 'It needs more time to recharge.'

I'm about to ask him exactly how long when the blue wall of the cell starts to bulge behind my dad's head.

'Look out!' I shout, pulling Dad away as the gleaming blue surface stretches and contorts. Then, with a sudden flubbery sound like a thousand rubber bands being pinged at once, a hideous creature emerges out of the blue.

A FATE WORSE THAN DEATH

It looks like a giant sea slug. The creature's translucent skin shimmers with bright, neon colours, whilst the bulbous bulk of its body towers above us both. As I look up in horror at the place where its face should be, I see a single probing tentacle staring back at me.

And then there's a terrible smell.

'Prisoners! The Cosmic Authority has sent me to escort you to your doom!'

These words boom inside my brain even though I can't see the mouth they're coming from. I turn to my dad in terror as a small puddle of slime slowly pools on the floor around the alien.

'How come it's speaking English?' I gasp.

'Er, it's not,' Dad replies, grimacing as he wipes a stray strand of slime from where it has splatted on his face. 'The Gezundhai communicate solely through their scent glands. They don't make speeches – they make smells. And the Quintessence translates these whiffy emissions into words inside our heads.'

'Silence!'

An even fouler smell rises up from the alien like a cloud of cow pies.

Then the electric blue wall begins to bulge again and, with a slippery popping sound, a second of these creatures enters the cell. This one is smaller than the first, not much taller than me, but apart from that the creatures look exactly the same.

With a phut-phut sound, a neon bubble rises from somewhere near the rear end of this smaller alien. It floats up into the air and then pops to release a ghastly smell.

As soon as the stench hits my nostrils, the alien's words appear directly in my head: 'I'm bored.'

Ignoring the smaller alien, the larger slug-like creature waves its protruding tentacle in the direction of my dad as another stinking puddle of slime washes towards us.

'You will follow me to the Chamber of Judgement,' it oozes, as the electric blue walls suddenly blink out of existence. 'There you will be sentenced for your terrible crime of trespassing on to a P-class planet and exposing the universe to their infectious ideas. Do not try to escape.'

I don't know about escaping, but I'm finding it difficult to breathe as the alien's noxious emissions waft over me.

'Please stop talking,' I gasp.

Then my dad lets out a small musical fart that quickly peters out into silence.

'Dad!'

'Sorry,' he says, wincing as if he's trying to remember exactly how the tune goes. 'My Gezundhai is a bit rusty now. Tell you what, I'll leave it to the Quintessence to do the translating.'

'Silence!' Another foul-smelling cloud rises up from the giant alien slug. 'You will follow me!'

We now seem to be standing in a vast cavernous corridor, its curving walls pulsing with an eerie glow. The slug-like creature slithers forward, its gelatinous body quivering in rhythmic waves as it leaves a trail of slime for us to follow.

'I'm afraid there's been a big mistake,' Day says, hurrying to catch up with the giant gastropod. 'You can take me to the Chamber of Judgement, but my son Jake shouldn't be here. He got himself beamed up by mistake.'

I feel a slimy tentacle poke me in the back and twist round to see the smaller of the slug-like creatures prodding me on. I hurry forward, my footsteps echoing off the metallic floor that gleams like blackened sunshine.

'Kids, eh?' The giant alien slug's words appear in a puff of curdled steam. 'They never listen, do they? Take this one here,' it exudes, waggling its eye-tentacle back in the direction of the smaller alien. 'It's "Bring Your Daughter to Work Day" today, but with all the fuss this one's been making you'd think it was "Torture Your Child at Work Day". *Stop fluorescing in front of my friends, Dad,* she said when I picked her up from her mum's, and since then it's been moan, moan, moan. *"Do I have to sing on the way to the cells? Do I have to shout at the prisoners so loud?"* Here I am, trying to show her the exciting life of an intergalactic guard and all she can say is she's bored!'

I glance over at the smaller slug-like creature as it slithers along beside me.

'Is that your dad?' I ask.

The slimy alien bobs its head, its translucent

skin now shimmering a crimson red.

'He's *so* embarrassing,' she replies in a rasp of stale air.

'See what I mean,' the giant slug continues, its jelly-like body wobbling as it slowly negotiates a curve in the corridor. 'No respect for their fathers. Think all that we're good for is pocket money and lifts home from interplanetary trips.'

My dad nods his head in agreement. 'It's the same for me too,' he says. 'When I picked him up from this year's school disco, Jake made me wait on the street outside. He said he didn't want me showing off my breakdancing moves like I did last year.'

I shudder as I remember the horror of the Year Five disco – Dad spinning on his head across the dance floor and then taking out my head teacher at the knees. Mr Ronson was off school for five weeks after that with a fractured femur.

'It's not breakdancing when you do it,' I mutter under my breath. 'It's broken dancing.'

Overhearing my muttered joke, the younger Gezundhai secretes a slimy trail of giggles in her wake.

'You know, it's almost a shame I've got to escort you to a fate worse than death,' the Gezundhai guard belches, spraying my dad with a shower of foul-smelling slime. 'I can't help thinking that you and I have got a lot in common. Two ordinary dads just trying to do the best we can.'

Dad wipes the slime from his face with the back of his sleeve. 'Perhaps you *don't* have to escort us to a fate worse than death,' he suggests, looking up at the giant slug with a hopeful smile. 'You could say we escaped and let us beam back down to Earth.'

'Oh no, no, no,' the guard guffs in reply. 'What kind of example would I be setting my daughter by doing that? No, I'll deliver you both to the Cosmic Authority and then I can clock off for lunch. I could murder some Dentrassi stew.'

Dad's shoulders sag as the giant slug slithers forward again, leading us to our doom.

I glance across at the guard's daughter, but she just waggles her eye-tentacle apologetically.

It's no good. We're being taken to the Chamber of Judgement to face a fate worse than death. And we're going to get there very, very slowly.

I fall into step next to my dad, the two of us shuffling forward and then stopping, shuffling forward and then stopping as the Gezundhai sluggishly oozes its way along the corridor.

'So what do we do now?' I hiss, frantically searching my brain for any kind of escape plan.

But before Dad can even think of replying, another foul-smelling cloud chokes him into—

'Silence!' The stinking pall hangs above the giant slug's head, its eye-tentacle swivelling in my direction. 'Or at least speak up a bit so I can hear you. I can't stand the way you young people mumble all the time.'

I sniff a sigh of exasperation from the

smaller Gezundhai behind me and, echoing this, thrust my hands deep into my pockets. I can't believe I'm being nagged by a giant alien slug. I sometimes used to wish that my own dad would nag me like this – telling me to tidy my room or get my homework done – just like an ordinary dad. But he never did.

I glance across at Dad, his bright green skin still looking so strange to me. I know now that he's far from ordinary, but I don't care any more. I don't want an ordinary dad. I just want to find a way to get us both home.

Inside my pocket I feel the smooth shape of the Quintessence nestling next to the socks I stuffed there before. And as my fingers touch these furry socks and the giant slug's eyestalk flicks back to the corridor ahead, this jogs a memory loose inside my mind.

I remember standing in the wings at the school concert and hear Damon's voice inside my head, telling me the best way to defeat a Dalek. *Stick a sock on their eyestalk and they can't see a thing*, he said. *For a master race of alien monsters, they're pretty rubbish really.*

Amba laughed at this idea at the time, but maybe this is the kind of crazy plan I need now to rescue my dad from the Gezundhai. But I'm going to have to be quick . . .

Nudging him in the ribs, I whisper to my dad out of the side of my mouth, 'Get ready to run.'

'Silence!' A fresh stink erupts from the giant slug leading the way, its eye-tentacle swivelling in my direction again. But this time I'm ready for it, drawing my weapons out of my pocket like a gunslinger stuck in a sock drawer.

With an acrobatic leap, I plant the first of these on top of the alien's eyestalk, blindfolding the giant slug creature with a polka-dot sock from Marks and Spencer.

'My vision is impaired!' The alien guard rears up on its tail, its gelatinous bulk quivering with rage.

Spinning round like I'm on stage at the

school concert, I spring backwards to plant the second of the socks on the smaller alien's eye-tentacle. She sniffs as if listening to the pong emanating from the sock and then sprays out a shriek.

'I can't see! And this thing reeks!'

As this stinking shower of slime rains down on us, I grab hold of Dad's hand.

'Let's get out of here!'

BiG, iSN'T iT?

Running away from smelly alien slugs turns out to be the easy part of the escape plan. As Dad and I dash down the cavernous corridor we soon leave the Gezundhai behind, a faint whiffed yell of 'Come back now!' clinging to our noses.

Our footsteps clatter off the metallic floor, the eerie lights that seem to track our path pulsing along the curving walls. I don't know where we're running to. I don't even know if we'll ever get there as the corridor seems to stretch on for ever.

'How do we get out of this place?' I ask, gasping out the words as I run.

'We've got to find an escape pod,' Dad replies. 'All intergalactic spaceships this size have one on every level. If we can find it then we'll be able to climb in and blast off back to Earth.'

He slows to a halt, his gaze snagging on a circular control panel that's fixed halfway up the wall.

'Just give me a second, Jake,' Dad calls out. 'I think this might be it.'

Grateful for a breather, I glance back nervously over my shoulder as Dad taps at the panel. Above my head I see the lights that have followed us along the corridor suddenly blink into darkness. Turning back in surprise, I then see the curved walls of the corridor in front of us start to slowly slide apart to reveal a glittering circle of stars.

At first I feel rush of panic, thinking that

maybe this is some kind of airlock that's going to blast me out into space, but then I feel Dad's hand on my shoulder.

'Don't worry,' he says, following my gaze as I watch the transparent bubble bulge outwards. 'It's completely safe. This is the escape pod – its shell is completely see-through. We just need to wait for the pressure to equalize before we can step inside.'

I don't believe it. Dad thinks we're going to escape into outer space inside a bubble. Does he think we can just float back to Earth?

But the impossibility of this idea fades into insignificance as I stare out into the widening darkness. I can see thousands of stars – no, millions of stars – all looking so much brighter than I've ever seen them before. Each piercing point of light gleams with an icy fire. And as I peer into the black spaces between these stars, I realize that this darkness is filled with even more stars. It looks like the entire universe is shining down on me.

'Big, isn't it?'

I nod my head, almost unable to speak, but then I realize what I can't see.

'Where's Earth?' I croak.

Peering out through the escape pod window as its widening circle comes to a halt, Dad points his finger towards a tiny blue dot, barely visible amongst the silent glitter of stars.

'That's Earth,' he says, his voice gentle in my ear. 'We must be out past Neptune by now.'

I stare at this pale blue dot, feeling so far from home. I can't see the land or the oceans, just a tiny blue speck all alone in the universe.

Then Dad puts his arm around my shoulder and suddenly I don't feel so alone.

'I always wanted to show you this, Jake,' he says. 'The universe is so beautiful and it belongs to you too. I always thought that one day I could take you to the stars, but I just wish it wasn't like this.'

As we stand there together, I can almost fool myself that we're back in our garden at home, staring up at the stars. Any minute now Mum will come to the back door and tell me that it's getting past my bedtime.

'That's it,' Dad says, as the transparent wall between us and the bubble starts to dissolve with a hiss.

But then I smell something rather unpleasant

and turn around to see a single eye-tentacle staring back at me through a hole in the sock.

'Surprise! Surprise!' the Gezundhai belches, and as the stinking spray hits my face, I feel the lights blink out inside my head. The last thing I hear before I hit the ground is Dad's voice calling out my name.

PREPARE TO MEET YOUR DOOM

'Jake!'

The sound of this voice seems to be coming from a million miles away, like some kind of broadcast from a distant star.

'Jake, are you OK?'

Opening my eyes, I sway gently from side to side trying to work out exactly how I can be standing on two feet if I've only just woken up. I blink, my gaze slowly focusing on Dad's face as he peers at me in concern. Even though my brain still feels fogged with sleep, I manage to croak out a question.

'What happened?'

'We got Gezundhai'd,' Dad explains, spitting on the corner of his handkerchief and using this to wipe my face.

'Dad!' I protest, trying to push his hand away.

'Stay still,' Dad says, smudging the hankie across my face. 'The Gezundhai can exude a paralysing anaesthetic agent in their mucus, this slime instantly knocking anyone unconscious on contact. That's what happened to us.' He pulls the handkerchief away from my face, its blue-checked pattern now dripping with slime. 'You'll feel better now.'

As Dad slips the sopping hankie into his pocket I do feel more awake, although I wish he'd used a wet wipe. Then I catch sight of what's behind Dad and gasp out loud in surprise.

We seem to be standing on the stage of some kind of vast theatre – a bit like the place Mrs Beale took my class to last Christmas to watch *Cinderella*. But instead of the rows of comfy red-cushioned seats that they have at the Palace Theatre in town, here I can see golden galleries ringing the stage, their endless rows rising upwards as they seem to stretch into infinity. And looking down from every glowing balcony, I can see *aliens*.

There must be tens of thousands of them, all looking so unearthly and strange. Most of the time on TV shows like *Doctor Who*, they make the aliens look kind of human. They might have pointy ears or green scaly skin or even tentacles where their faces should be, but they look human-*ish*. But most of the things I can see here look so far from human . . .

Bird-like skeletons perch on the edge of the nearest gallery, their bony beaks opening wide as I watch. Above them, I see a blob that seems to be made of living spaghetti, the writhing worms of its body constantly changing shape. My eyes flick upwards, unable to take in what I'm looking at. Creatures made of rock, crystal

and clouds, every shape even stranger than the last. There are tentacles and antennae, claws and pincers, shells and suckers and teeth. And in amongst this outlandish alien zoo, I catch a glimpse of the odd human form, sometimes with bright green skin just like Dad, but then they're gone, lost in a swarm of strange insect creatures whose multi-coloured bodies bristle with stings.

'Where are we?' I murmur.

'I think this must be the Chamber of Judgement,' Dad says, his voice trembling as the strangest-looking chandelier I've ever seen starts to float down from the domed roof. 'And that is the Cosmic Authority.'

I stare upwards in disbelief. The glowing creature looks like a glass sculpture of a squid, its shimmering tentacles trailing light as it descends. It's as big as a bus, if a bus had a huge bulbous head, funnel-shaped body and more than a dozen tentacles and arms. It seems to be completely transparent, but then the creature opens its enormous eyes and I see two silvery moons staring down at me.

I can't believe this is really an alien. It looks more like a work of art.

'What is it?' I ask.

'The Cosmic Authority is a Photophore,' my dad explains, his voice hushed as the alien creature hangs suspended in the air. 'One of the oldest civilizations in the galaxy and the guardians of its laws. Photophores are bioluminescent – they speak in the language of light.'

As if to prove Dad's words right, a ripple of light pulses through the Cosmic Authority's form. This blue-green flash travels to the tips of its tentacles and, with the Quintessence still in my pocket, I find I can understand what it's saying perfectly.

'WELCOME TO THE CHAMBER OF JUDGEMENT,' the Cosmic Authority glares. 'PREPARE TO MEET YOUR DOOM.'

That doesn't mean I like what it's saying.

Another firework display shimmers through the translucent squid, the colours flashing red, green and gold.

'ION OF MMBOGBJSQXMMHXZOHZMMHPHF-SZDIXZSOESPCXMMMMBOUZTJMJPHPHPHPDI, YOU STAND ACCUSED OF BREAKING THE LAWS OF THE UNIVERSE. TRESPASSING INTO THE COSMIC ZONE OF EXCLUSION, LANDING ON A P-CLASS WORLD, DISGUISING YOURSELF AS A HUMAN BEING NAMED "ION JONES" AND ALLOWING YOURSELF TO BE IN-FECTED BY THEIR PRIMITIVE WAYS. HOW DO YOU PLEAD?'

The huge silvery moons of its eyes shine fierce and bright and my dad seems to shrink beneath the Cosmic Authority's gaze. I stare up in awe at this creature of light, holding my breath as I wait for Dad to say something that'll make things all right.

There's a moment of silence, the eyestalks and antennae of every creature inside the vast Chamber of Judgement turned towards my dad. And then I hear his muttered reply.

'Guilty, I suppose.'

'Dad!'

Glancing in my direction, Dad waves me into silence with a desperate look.

'But I had a good reason for breaking these laws,' Dad pleads, turning his gaze back towards the fluorescing space squid. 'I thought I was answering a distress call that came from the direction of planet Earth. A message from a stranded traveller who said he was lost, floating somewhere above this blue world. I was just trying to help.'

In reply, a silvery flush ripples through the creature's tentacles.

'YOU LIE!' The Cosmic Authority's words fall in a shower of terrifying sparks, each one dripping with contempt. 'PLANET EARTH HAS BEEN PLACED IN A SPHERE OF SILENCE. ALL SIGNALS BLOCKED TO PREVENT THE CIVILIZED UNIVERSE FROM BEING INFECTED BY THEIR AGGRESSION. THIS BACKWARDS WORLD HAS BEEN MUTED! YOU HEARD NO DISTRESS CALL.'

'Well, you see, that's the thing,' Dad says with a frightened laugh. 'I found out it wasn't really a distress call. It was a song. You see, the humans make music. Not the music of the spheres that we hear out here in space – the rhythmic roar of a plasma wave or the pulsing beat of a neutron star – but songs that tell us what it means to be alive. This was the most beautiful song I'd ever heard. And a human being had made it. I thought if they were capable of this, then maybe they weren't as primitive as we thought they were. I had to stay to find out more . . .' Dad's voice trails away into a whisper. 'I fell in love.'

The Cosmic Authority's body lights up like a disapproving Catherine wheel.

'YOU ARE INFECTED!' it blazes. 'BABBLING ABOUT THESE THINGS CALLED SONGS WHEN WE KNOW THIS PLANET IS CAPABLE ONLY OF CRUELTY. AS PUNISHMENT FOR YOUR CRIMES, YOU WILL BE SENT INTO EXILE ON THE EVENT HORIZON OF THE NEAREST BLACK HOLE. AN ETERNAL WARNING TO

ALL THOSE WHO DARE TO BREAK THE LAWS OF THE UNIVERSE.'

Dad's mouth falls open in shock at this sentence. He closes and then opens his mouth several times as if trying to reply, but no words come out.

'GUARDS!' The Cosmic Authority's tentacles ignite with an eerie red glow. 'TAKE HIM AWAY.'

From behind me, I hear the familiar slithering sounds of the Gezundhai.

I can't let this happen.

'No!' I cry, shouting up at the giant space squid. 'If you want to send my dad into a black hole, then you're going to have to get past me first.'

The Cosmic Authority flicks a tentacle in my direction and I watch as a shimmering beam of light ripples across my hand. The green hue that saturated my skin before is now completely gone and this light flickers through the colours of the rainbow before turning to a brilliant white.

'**YOU ARE A HUMAN BEING,**' the Cosmic Authority shimmers, its tentacles recoiling in fear. '**YOU SHOULD NEVER HAVE BEEN BROUGHT HERE. THIS MISTAKE WILL BE CORRECTED. YOU WILL BE RETURNED TO EARTH. ALONE.**'

'Jake,' Dad grabs hold of my hand. 'It's no use protesting – you have to go back. I need to know that you're safe.'

'I won't go back without you,' I sob. Pulling my hand free, I shake my fist at the shimmering alien. 'If you try and send me back, I'll tell everyone the truth. About my dad and the aliens and your stupid Cosmic Zone of Exclusion – I'll tell the truth about everything.'

The Cosmic Authority's tentacles glow with a rainbow light.

'**YOU WILL NOT REMEMBER THE TRUTH,**' it explains. '**ALL THIS WILL BE WIPED FROM YOUR MIND, ALONG WITH ALL MEMORIES OF "ION JONES". IN FACT, ION JONES WILL BE WIPED FROM THE MEMORIES OF EVERYONE ON EARTH. IT WILL BE AS IF HE WAS NEVER THERE. THE SPHERE OF SILENCE**

WILL BE STRENGTHENED AND WE WILL LEAVE YOUR PLANET TO STEW IN ITS IGNORANCE.'

I stare up at the shimmering tentacles as these words sink into my brain.

The Cosmic Authority doesn't just want to take my dad – it wants to take all my memories of him too.

I shake my head as the memories come rushing in: Dad dancing at the disco, jumping on stage at the school concert, every embarrassing moment I've ever wanted to forget. But then I remember all the other times too. How he helped me to build the best ever den. How he makes my favourite treats for our Saturday-night movie marathons. All the times we've played together, laughed together and the way he always makes Mum smile. All those times I snuggled close under the crook of Dad's arm as we stared up at the stars.

And the Cosmic Authority wants to steal all these moments from me with a swish of its tentacles.

There's only one way I can stop this.

'You can't do this to me,' I cry, fumbling in my pocket as I search for the one thing that will help me. 'You can't send me back.'

'YOU MUST GO BACK,' the Cosmic Authority gleams, its words shimmering with scorn. **'YOU ARE A HUMAN BEING.'**

I shake my head. 'I'm not.'

With trembling hands, I hold the Quintessence aloft, the starry lights on the device now shining brightly again. Dad was right – it just needed time to recharge. Then I twist the device between my fingers and feel myself start to change.

DANCING OUT IN SPACE

It starts as a tingle in the palm of my hand, a strange fizzing sensation that seems to seep into my veins. Then this dizzying rush floods right through me. It feels like my body is pulsing with flashing colours, but this light is all on the inside. The Quintessence is reprogramming my biology – changing me back to what I was before. I feel different, but the same. I'm becoming *me* again.

As the lights on the Quintessence slowly fade into darkness, I stare up at the Cosmic

Authority.

'What do your scanners say I am now?'

With a puzzled glare, the space squid flicks its tentacle towards me again. I watch as another ray of light ripples across my skin, but this time the light doesn't stop changing, the shimmering beam constantly flickering between the colours of the rainbow.

'I . . . I DON'T KNOW,' the Cosmic Authority blinks.

'My dad comes from another planet, but my mum comes from Earth. So what does that make me?' I half smile as I remember what Amba said when Damon asked this same question. 'Half human? Half alien? Am I infected or in need of protection? Should I be inside or outside your stupid Zone of Exclusion?'

In reply to my question, the creature's body turns completely transparent. It doesn't seem to want to answer me, but I've got to make it understand.

'You say my dad is "infected" by Earth's

primitive ways, but he really just fell in love –
with its songs, with its music, with my mum.
If he hadn't trespassed on planet Earth, then I
wouldn't be here. I used to feel like I didn't fit
in sometimes and wondered why this was, but
now I know exactly who I am.' With my hearts
thumping in my chest, I take a deep breath.
'Jake Jones of number twelve Ashcroft Road,
Pendleton, Manchester, England, Great Britain,
Europe, the Earth, the Solar System, the Milky
Way, the Universe.'

I glance across at my dad and see tears
shining in his eyes.

'The only crime my dad is guilty of is being
a bit embarrassing sometimes, but that doesn't
mean he deserves to be dumped on the edge of a
black hole. I used to think I wanted an ordinary
dad, but now I know why I'm lucky to have a
dad who's out of this world. It's not because
he's an alien, it's because he's always told me
that you can be whatever you want to be – a
gymnast, a Jedi Knight, even a rock star!'

'That's right, Jake,' Dad says, reaching out to take my hand. Mine's still pink whilst his is green, but I know we're both the same.

'Keeping Earth in a Cosmic Zone of Exclusion is wrong,' I say, raising my voice so everyone can hear. 'We're part of the universe too and it's cruel to keep us alone. I know you think the human race is primitive – and maybe it is sometimes – but there's so much more to the people on Earth than the things you hear on the news. That only tells you what's going wrong in the world, but there are so many people trying to imagine a better world too. You'll find this in the stories we share and the songs that we sing. These are the things that show what it really means to be human.'

Suspended in the air, the glowing shape of the Cosmic Authority still looks like solid glass. I look around the Chamber of Judgement, strange alien faces peering down at me from every gallery.

'If you listened to these, you might learn

something . . .'

My voice trails away. I don't know what else I can say. How can I make them see that I'm telling them the truth?

Then I realize, I don't need to make them see – they just need to *listen*.

I turn towards my dad, holding up the Quintessence in my hand.

'You said this was the heart of your spaceship,' I say. 'Does that mean it will have a record of the signal you received that brought you to Earth twelve years ago?'

Dad nods his head, a sudden gleam appearing in his blue-green eyes. 'Play communication channel records,' he says, talking to the Quintessence like it's the smart speaker at home. 'Message received T-minus twelve Sol orbits ago.'

Strange lights flicker across the surface of the pebble-shaped device, like tiny black stars in the night. Then I hear the familiar sound of some strummed guitar chords.

'Full volume,' Dad says with a twinkle in his eye and the sound from the Quintessence swells to fill the Chamber of Judgement.

'**WHAT IS THIS?**' the Cosmic Authority demands, its tentacles flashing red in warning.

'A song,' I shout, raising my voice above the rising chords and the martial beat of a snare drum. 'A song that shows you what it means to be alone.'

Then I hear David Bowie start to sing, telling the story of Major Tom as he lifts off into space.

I look around the vast chamber as 'Space Oddity' rings out. The strange alien faces that fill the endless galleries seem transfixed, swaying in time with the chiming melody as the Quintessence's circuits translate the singer's words into an infinity of alien languages.

Dad squeezes my hand as we listen to the song and I glance up to meet his gaze.

'This is our song too, Jake,' he says with a smile. 'Fancy joining in?'

Staring up into Dad's blue-green eyes, I hear the song start to lift off. There's no time to be embarrassed any more. The only thing left to do is sing.

I nod my head.

'Let's do it.'

As the aliens watch we join in with David Bowie, Dad throwing his best rock star shapes as we sing about floating in space and how different the stars look today. From the galleries I see a forest of tentacles and antennae, all swaying in time with the song.

Dad always wanted to be the biggest star in the universe

and it looks like he's finally made it.

The song is spiralling to a close, the singer telling us about this blue planet called Earth and how there's nothing left that he can do. I realize now why Dad thought this was a distress call. It really sounds like the loneliest voice in the universe, begging to be heard.

And as the last notes of the song sweep into silence, I stare up at the Cosmic Authority. A flickering pulse seems to flow through its tentacles. Then I hear a strange ringing noise. It sounds like the chimes of some strange kind of alien bell, the sound of this coming from every corner of the chamber.

'What's that noise?' I ask, turning to Dad in alarm. 'What's happening?'

But Dad just grins back at me. 'They're cheering, Jake.'

As the cheers ring out the Cosmic Authority descends, its tentacles shimmering with the same chiming light. It's floating right in front of me now, its huge silvery eyes seeming to peer right inside my mind.

'I'M SORRY,' it begins with an apologetic flicker of its tentacles. 'I DIDN'T UNDERSTAND BEFORE, BUT THIS SONG HAS SHOWN ME HOW WRONG I HAVE BEEN.'

'So you'll set us free?' I ask, a new hope fluttering in my chest.

The shimmering space squid raises a single long tentacle, an emerald pulse of light flashing to the very tip of this.

'YES,' it replies. 'I WILL RETURN YOU BOTH TO PLANET EARTH, BUT ON ONE CONDITION.'

'What's that?' Dad asks, scarcely able to believe what he's hearing.

Another firework display of lights pulses through the space squid's body.

'YOU KEEP PLAYING THE SONGS.'

'I don't understand,' I say, but the Cosmic Authority starts to explain with a wave of its tentacles.

'FOR US, THIS IS A NEW FORM OF COMMUNI-CATION. THE SONG THAT YOU PLAYED SHOWED ME

SO MUCH ABOUT THE HUMAN RACE. IT TOLD ME
ABOUT YOUR COURAGE AND KINDNESS, THE WAY
YOU LOVE ONE ANOTHER AND HOW IT FEELS TO BE
ALONE. BUT IT DID SOMETHING ELSE TOO. IT MADE
US FEEL CONNECTED TO YOU.'

As the Cosmic Authority fluoresces, I hear the echo of Mum's words as she told me why Dad loves to sing: *Everyone's connected when they hear the song*. Even across the universe it seems.

The space squid's glowing tentacles draw an imploring pattern in the air.

'PLEASE PLAY US MORE OF THESE SONGS.'

Dad's eyes goggle in amazement. 'You're making us intergalactic DJs?' he splutters.

The Cosmic Authority lights up like a neon bulb.

'THE SPHERE OF SILENCE PLACED AROUND THE
EARTH WILL BE MODIFIED AND A SINGLE CHANNEL
PROVIDED FOR YOU TO TRANSMIT ON. IF THINGS GO
WELL, IN TIME, THE TRANSMISSIONS WILL BECOME
TWO-WAY. WE WILL SHARE OUR KNOWLEDGE WITH

THE HUMAN RACE, WHILST YOU SHARE YOUR SONGS WITH US.'

The Cosmic Authority turns its gaze towards me, the silvery moons of its eyes shining bright as rainbow pulses of light shimmer across its tentacles.

'SO WHAT DO YOU SAY, JAKE?' the alien asks. 'WILL YOU HELP US LEARN WHAT IT MEANS TO BE HUMAN?'

I stare into these silvery moons and see my own reflection looking back at me. Human? Alien? It doesn't matter. It's what you *do* that counts.

'Of course,' I tell the Cosmic Authority with a grin. I glance up at the glowing balconies to see the aliens, all peering back at me. 'And I'll make sure the songs we play get you dancing out in space.'

TWELVE MINUTES LATER . . .

WE'RE NOT ALONE

I can see the TV news crews still camped outside my house, the camera lights that illuminate the pavement outside my front gate so bright that nobody noticed the brief flash of light that beamed Dad and me back down in the middle of Ashcroft Road.

I hop from toe to toe as I wait for the effects of teleportation to wear off, my dad doing the same silent dance before the pain eventually fades away.

Glancing up I see the silent darkness of the

Cosmic Authority's ship disappearing into the night, the stars coming out again one by one.

'Are you ready?' Dad asks me.

I glance across to meet his gaze. He's still dressed in his ridiculous silver ski suit, but at least Dad's used the Quintessence to change his skin back from being bright green. We don't want to create any kind of international crisis about an alien invasion.

I nod my head.

'Ready,' I reply with a smile. 'Let's go home.'

We start walking, making our way past the outside broadcast vans parked along the street and we're almost at the front gate before the camera crews notice that we're there.

'It's them!'

As the camera operators scramble for position, the reporters jump into life, firing out questions as Dad pushes open the gate.

'Was that really a UFO?'

'Can you tell us where you've been?'

'Is this all some kind of hoax?'

I follow my dad, ignoring the camera flashes as the front door opens and I see Mum start running down the garden path to greet us, Damon and Amba grinning wildly as they follow close behind. But before I take another step forward I feel a hand on my arm, pulling me back.

I turn around and, leaning over the garden gate, Asha Barnes thrusts a microphone into my face.

'Jake,' she asks, her expression deadly serious. 'Are we alone in the universe?'

I look down the camera lens that's hovering over her shoulder. I think about what I saw on the Cosmic Authority's spaceship: glowing squids and smelly space slugs, the endless galleries filled with strange alien races all swaying in time with the song. I remember staring at the stars glittering in the dark, each one a sun with planets spinning round it, just like ours. I felt really small then, but I wasn't alone.

I shake my head with a smile.

'No,' I reply, the word almost popping out of me as my family and friends wrap their arms around me in a hug. 'We're not alone.'

Acknowledgements

In 1950, the physicist Enrico Fermi posed a question that has intrigued scientists to this day. Given the size of our galaxy, the Milky Way, which contains billions of stars, and the chances that many of these stars could have Earth-like planets orbiting them, and that many of these planets could have developed intelligent civilizations, maybe in advance of our own, with the power to travel across the galaxy, Fermi asked one simple question, 'So where are they?'. This simple question became known as the Fermi paradox and many scientists have come up with theories to try to explain why we haven't yet found any evidence for the existence of alien life. In *Space Oddity*, I tried to write a story that provided one possible answer to this question and I'd like to thank the authors of the following books for helping me to understand more about humanity's search for extraterrestrial intelligence: *Human*

Universe by Professor Brian Cox and Andrew Cohen, *The Aliens Are Coming!* by Ben Miller and *Aliens* edited by Jim Al-Khalili.

Music also plays a very important part in the story, especially the songs of David Bowie, but I'd like to thank all the musicians who helped write the soundtrack to the writing of this book, especially Tim Burgess, whose Twitter listening parties reminded me of the immense power music has to bring us together.

Sincerest thanks to Ben Mantle for his wonderful cover art and illustrations. Huge thanks too to all the team at Chicken House, especially Rachel Leyshon, Rachel Hickman, Esther Waller, Elinor Bagenal and Barry Cunningham. And thank you too to my brilliant agent, Lucy Juckes.

Finally, I'd like to thank my family for all their love, support and understanding, especially my wonderful wife, Chrissie. I love you very much, you know.

MILTON THE MIGHTY by EMMA READ
Illustrated by ALEX G GRIFFITHS

When spider Milton discovers he's been branded deadly, he fears for his life and his species.
Alongside his buddies, big hairy Ralph and daddy-long-legs Audrey, he decides to clear his name. But to succeed, Milton must befriend his house human, Zoe. Is Milton mighty enough to achieve the impossible?

'. . . a charming and thoughtful read.'
THE SCOTSMAN

Paperback, ISBN 978-1-911490-81-4, £6.99 • ebook, ISBN 978-1-912626-31-1, £6.99

WHO LET THE GODS OUT? by MAZ EVANS

When Elliot wished upon a star, he didn't expect a constellation to crash into his dungheap. Virgo thinks she's perfect. Elliot doesn't. Together they release Thanatos, evil Daemon of Death. Epic fail.

They need the King of the Gods and his noble steed. They get a chubby Zeus and his high horse Pegasus.

Are the Gods really ready to save the world? And is the world really ready for the Gods?

'. . . lashings of adventure, the Olympic gods as you've never seen them before and a wonderfully British sense of humour.'
FIONA NOBLE, THE BOOKSELLER

Paperback, ISBN 978-1-910655-41-2, £6.99 • ebook, ISBN 978-1-910655-64-1, £6.99

BEETLE BOY by M. G. LEONARD

Darkus can't believe his eyes when a huge insect drops out of the trouser leg of his horrible new neighbour. It's a giant beetle – and it seems to want to communicate.

But how can a boy be friends with a beetle? And what does a beetle have to do with the disappearance of his dad and the arrival of Lucretia Cutter, with her taste for creepy jewellery?

'A darkly funny Dahl-esque adventure.'
KATHERINE WOODFINE, AUTHOR

Paperback, ISBN 978-1-910002-70-4, £6.99 • ebook, ISBN 978-1-910002-98-8, £6.99